MW01140212

BITTER END

A Dr. Beckett Campbell Medical Examiner Thriller

Book 0

Patrick Logan

Books by Patrick Logan

Detective Damien Drake

Book 1: Butterfly Kisses (feat. Chase Adams, Dr. Campbell)
Book 2: Cause of Death (feat. Chase Adams, Dr. Campbell)
Book 3: Download Murder (feat. Chase Adams, Dr. Campbell)
Book 4: Skeleton King (feat. Dr. Campbell)
Book 5: Human Traffic (feat. Dr. Campbell)
Book 6: Drug Lord: Part I
Book 7: Drug Lord: Part II

Chase Adams FBI Thrillers

Book 1: Frozen Stiff
Book 2: Shadow Suspect
Book 3: Drawing Dead
Book 4: Amber Alert (feat. Dr. Beckett Campbell)
Book 4.5: Georgina's Story
Book 5: Dirty Money
Book 6: Devil's Den

Dr. Beckett Campbell Medical Thrillers

Book 0: Bitter End
Book 1: Organ Donor
Book 2: Injecting Faith
Book 3: Surgical Precision

This book is a work of fiction. Names, characters, places, and incidents in this book are either entirely imaginary or are used fictitiously. Any resemblance to actual people, living or dead, or of places, events, or locales is entirely coincidental.

Copyright © Patrick Logan 2018
Interior design: © Patrick Logan 2018
All rights reserved.

This book, or parts thereof, cannot be reproduced, scanned, or disseminated in any print or electronic form.

First Edition: June 2018

Prologue

WITH A GROAN, DR. Beckett Campbell opened his eyes. His head was pounding, his eyelids felt gummy, and his balls... well, his balls were chaffed.

"What the fuck happened last night?" he grumbled.

Beckett managed to roll onto his side, wiping the half-caked puddle of drool from his cheek as he did.

Blinking rapidly helped clear the gunk that glued his eyelashes together, but he was still struggling to catch his bearings. The inside of his mouth tasted like a porcupine's asshole and he could barely swallow without retching. Even breathing in the sour smell of rum that seemed to be exuding from his very pores threatened to curdle his stomach. There was something else in the air, as well: something foul, something bitter.

Beckett forced himself to a seated position and then immediately froze.

What the fuck?

To his surprise, there was a woman lying on the bed beside him. She was completely nude and, despite his epic hangover, Beckett couldn't help but give her a once-over. Her ample breasts were pushed into the mattress as was her face, the latter covered in dark brown hair that swirled about the pillow. But it was her ass that held his attention the longest. It was tanned and firm, big but not overly so.

Just the way he liked it: hard enough to bounce quarters off, but not so muscled that it could crack walnuts.

Despite feeling like a dumpster full of diapers, Beckett felt a smile creep onto his face.

Well, that explains the chaffing on my balls, he thought with a chuckle.

Beckett was about to reach over and shake the woman awake, when for the second time in as many minutes, he stopped cold.

There was *another* woman lying beside the first. And, like tanned ass, she too was completely nude. She had blond hair instead of brown, but her ass was just as fabulous.

Beckett shook his head in admiration.

"You sly dog, you," he said to himself. Unlike his two female companions, Beckett wasn't naked; he sported a pair of bright red boxer briefs and nothing else.

After observing the women for a few moments longer, and feeling a stirring inside said boxers, Beckett reached out and laid a gentle hand on the blond woman's shoulder.

"Wake up," he said quietly, wondering if, despite his hangover, he might be able to perform again. Shit, he *had* to perform again; it was a crying shame that he recalled nothing of the night prior.

I'll give it the good ol' college try. Ma would be so proud.

"Wake up," Beckett repeated, this time shaking the woman a little more vigorously.

When she still failed to groan, let alone move, the smile slid off his face. Brow furrowed now, Beckett was about to reach for the other girl, the brunette, when there was a knock at his bedroom door.

Beckett paused, confusion washing over him.

Is this my *room?* he wondered. *All the rooms in the villa look the same. Correction, all the rooms in all the* villas *look the same.*

The voice that followed the knocking did nothing to clear up the confusion. If anything, it only added to it.

"*Policia!* Open up! *Policia!*"

Beckett's eyes bulged.

What the fuck? The police? Here?

"You gotta wake up," Beckett urged, shaking the blond woman with both hands now. His clouded mind conjured scenarios in which the two beautiful women on his bed had mobbed up boyfriends or had been promised to a Caribbean prince or something equally as unfortunate for him. "C'mon, wake up." His eyes darted to the window behind him that was half open. "You gotta get up and get outta here."

The only response was the splintering door as it exploded inward. Beckett immediately hopped to his feet, momentarily relieved that the three men who burst into his room appeared to be actual police officers and not overprotective boyfriends playing a role. Or strippers. *Male* strippers. It wouldn't have been his first choice, but if the good doctor had one motto, it was: *don't knock it 'til you try it.*

Snap out of it, Beckett, he scolded himself.

His relief was short-lived, however, when he noticed the barrels of their automatic weapons aimed directly at his tattooed chest.

Beckett's hands shot into the air and he said the first thing that came to mind, no matter how idiotic it sounded.

"I'm a doctor! Holy shit! Don't shoot, I'm a doctor!"

His credentials did nothing to soften the police officers' hard expressions, nor did it convince them to lower their guns—not that he really expected it to.

"Against the wall," one of the officers ordered in a thick accent.

Beckett did as he was instructed, moving away from the bed and backing up. A cool breeze ushered in through the window, finally offering him some solace from the stale bedroom air.

But while this served to clear his nostrils, his mind remained foggy.

What in the holy fuck is going on here?

Judging by his headache and the raw interior of his nose, Beckett figured he'd drunk a lot and snorted a little, but not remembering *anything*? Not remembering a night with the two beauties lying on his bed?

It had been a long while since he'd been that smashed.

And then there was that strange, bitter taste in his mouth...

One of the officers made his way to the bed, his eyes flicking from one naked woman to the other. The man's eyes lingered on their asses for just a second longer than a rudimentary glance, which, despite everything, caused Beckett to smirk. Then the officer bent down and put two fingers against the side of the brunette's throat. He waited for several seconds—all of them did, including Beckett—and then withdrew his hand and shook his head.

Beckett had no fucking idea what was going on, but he knew what *that* meant. *That* gesture was universal: *no mas* pulse.

"No," Beckett moaned softly, unable to control himself.

The officer who had checked the woman's pulse used the same two fingers to tease her dark hair away from her face.

Beckett's breath caught in his throat and he felt his heart fall into the pit of his stomach.

The woman's eyes were open, but her expression was completely blank. At the corners of her lips—beautiful, full lips, Beckett noted—was a thick, white paste.

He watched in horror as the officer repeated these actions with the blond girl.

Her lips were also caked with paste, her eyes blank.

No mas pulse.

They were both dead.

The two other officers who, up until this point, had been pointing their assault rifles at Beckett's chest, raised their aim a little higher.

And just when Beckett thought things couldn't get any stranger, any more terrifying, another man stepped into the room.

Only this man was clearly *not* a police officer.

But he was familiar to Beckett.

"Looks like you just couldn't stay out of trouble, could you, my good doctor?" the man said with a grin.

PART I

Coconuts and G-Strings

THIRTY-SIX HOURS AGO

Chapter 1

"A MUSHROOM WALKS INTO a bar and takes a seat. As the bartender approaches, the mushroom looks at the man sitting across from him and says, *I'll have whatever he's having*. The bartender looks down the bar, then turns his eyes back to the mushroom. *I'm sorry, but we don't serve your kind here*. The mushroom huffs. *Why not, I'm a fungi.*"

When there was no response, Beckett cleared his throat.

"*Fungi,*" he repeated. "Get it? *Fungi? Fun-guy?*"

"Oh," the bartender replied with half a grin.

"Oh—all I get is an *Oh*. Okay, Rodney Dangerfield, just hook me up with whatever she's having," Beckett said, casting a glance at the beautiful brunette wearing what might've been the world's smallest bikini. Seriously, dental floss was to slack lines as this bikini was to coverage area.

The woman, sensing his stare, raised her eyes, a smirk on her pretty face.

Maybe she'll like my jokes, he thought. But then his friend Drake's words echoed in his head.

No one likes your jokes, Beckett. They're like a cross between dad jokes and a Dr. Seuss train wreck.

Beckett resisted the urge to give the woman a wink and offered a subtle nod instead.

You're an asshole, Drake.

"You don't want one of those," the bartender whispered, leaning toward Beckett. "Trust me."

Beckett's eyes shifted from the woman's face to the coconut clutched in her manicured hand. A pink umbrella and an oversized lime-green straw poked out of the hacked-off top.

"The drink or the girl? *Ha,* kidding; you're probably right. Just some rum on the rocks, then."

The bartender smacked the bar with his palm, drawing Beckett's attention away from the woman. The man was lean and muscular, and his skin was deeply tanned. His eyes were a curiously light shade of brown and when they landed on Beckett, they didn't so much look *at* him as they did *through* him. This was mildly unsettling, and yet, at the same time, the bartender had the classic look of a young man who had traveled to the islands to escape something back home—an abusive father, maybe, or something less exciting, like overdue cell phone bills—and had simply never gone back.

"This your first time here?" the man asked, as he turned to fetch Beckett his drink. He had a slight accent, one that he had clearly worked hard at trying to rid himself of, which made it difficult for Beckett to place. It sounded like a cross between New York and Boston, but with its own subtle twang.

Eastern Canada, maybe, Beckett thought. *Halifax, Fredericton, or maybe even somewhere in Newfoundland. They had fucked-up accents in Newfoundland.*

"First time here, yep. In fact, this is the first vacation I've had in… shit, I don't know how long. Twelve years, maybe,"

Beckett said absently. Although he was conversing with the bartender—he knew the value of being on the man's good side should the resort unexpectedly become busy—his mind was on the woman at the other end of the bar.

We don't serve your kind here... we service *them.*

"That long, eh?" the bartender asked, sliding a glass of rum to Beckett.

"That long," Beckett confirmed, casting a glance down at himself.

It appeared as if he wasn't the only one practicing polite banter; with skin the color of unleavened dough, a paleness that not even the many tattoos that covered his chest and arms could mask, it was painfully obvious that many years passed since Beckett's flesh had been kissed by the sun.

The truth was, despite the warm sun and beautiful surroundings, Beckett didn't want to be here; he wanted to be back in New York doing what he did best: acting as the Senior Medical Examiner for the NYPD.

And tormenting young residents at NYU.

But it hadn't been up to him, not really. Not after what had happened to Craig Sloan.

A break... take a vacation, Beckett. Get some sun and clear your head, the goons from Internal Affairs had "suggested."

Beckett took a large gulp of his rum, then raised his eyes. He was surprised to find that the woman with the coconut was still staring at him.

Well, maybe vacations aren't all *bad,* he thought, rising to his feet. *And so long as I'm here, what's the harm in having a little fun?*

***

"Seriously? *You're* a doctor?"

Beckett took another sip of his rum and ran a hand through his bleach-blond hair before answering.

"What, you don't believe me? I don't *look* like a doctor to you?"

The brunette from the bar, who had since introduced herself as Chloe, leaned back and looked him up and down.

"Honestly?"

Beckett shrugged.

"Sure."

"Then, no. You look more like a rock star than a doctor."

Beckett allowed himself a small smile.

Rock star, huh? Could be worse...

"I'm okay with that. Besides, the only doctors who want to *look* like doctors are assholes, anyway," he said with a smirk. "But enough about me. What about you? What do you do that affords you the freedom to come to a place like this?"

Chloe's perfect lips wrapped around a green straw that extended out of the coconut.

"I'm a model," she replied after swallowing, and Beckett cringed. It wasn't that he doubted the woman—she was indeed attractive enough to be a model—but her campy reply reminded him of LA girls who all wanted to be actresses, but more often than not ended up as strippers or in porn.

And if he had to bet, Beckett would have put his money on the latter.

"Lots of modeling opportunities around here?" he asked, eyebrow raised.

It was a thinly-veiled joke; after all, they were on a semi-private island in the Caribbean, and Barracuda Point was as exclusive as it was expensive. In fact, if it weren't for his friend who managed the joint, and that it was the off-season, there was no way that even Beckett would have been able to afford a week stay.

"No, not really," Chloe replied, clearly not catching the joke. "I came down here with my manager on his boat—his yacht. Needed to stopover for a few days, refuel or something like that. Anyways, he said he would have some work for me in a week or so." She shrugged and held up the coconut. "And in the meantime, I get free drinks and some beautiful weather, you know? So, I'm not complaining."

"Amen to that," Beckett said, raising his own glass. "And is it just you here? You and your—" he resisted using the word pimp, "—manager? Or did you bring friends?"

Something crossed over Chloe's face then, something that could have been jealousy or something else entirely.

"Yeah, Donnie brought some friends—more models."

Although this news seemed to upset Chloe, it did quite the opposite for Beckett.

He didn't want to be here, but when the options were prison or a vacation at a luxury resort, what choice did he have?

After all, even though he was never one to shy away from new experiences, a skinny, white boy like him, even with his tattoos, wouldn't fare well in prison. Even his rudimentary knowledge of jiu-jitsu would only get him so far when his cellmates were dead set on making him the cream in their Oreo.

But now… sharing the resort with Chloe and her friends? It could be worse.

Much worse.

"And your boss—you say he's got a boat? What kind of—"

A hand came down on Beckett's shoulder and he immediately grabbed the wrist—a man's wrist—and pulled forward while at the same time, standing and twisting. The man who had accosted him was slight, and he slammed awkwardly against the table.

Chloe yelped as Beckett continued to twist the man's arm. But when he recognized the goatee, the narrow nose, and wide-set eyes, he let go and took a step back.

"Screech?" Beckett said, making a face. "What the fuck are you doing here?"

Stephen "Screech" Thompson rose to his feet and rubbed his wrist.

"What the hell, man? A little jumpy, are we?"

Beckett chuckled to himself. His mind had been going over worst-case prison scenarios when Screech had touched him.

That was never a good time to say hello with a back slap.

"I'm sorry—had my mind in the clouds. What the hell are you doing here? Did Drake send you to check up on me? What a sweetheart, that guy."

Screech opened his mouth to answer when he noticed Chloe staring at them, a confused look on her face.

"I'll tell you later," Screech said with a goofy grin. "Why don't you introduce me to your friend first?"

Chapter 2

"IT WAS NICE TO meet both of you," Chloe said, rising to her feet. She wobbled briefly, and Beckett placed a hand on the small of her back for support. "But I need to get going. Donnie said he wanted to take some more photos before sunset. I'll be back here around seven-thirty... either that or on the boat. You should join me."

"You need an escort?" Beckett offered.

Chloe shook her head.

"I'll be fine," she replied. They were so close now that Beckett could smell her breath, which was strangely bitter.

"You sure?"

Chloe nodded and Beckett pulled his hand away, ready to steady her again should his support be needed. But, true to her word, the woman straightened and then started to walk away from them, her gait, while not completely adroit, more stable now.

Both Screech and Beckett watched her go with something akin to reverence. Even when Chloe had disappeared behind one of the villas, the two men continued to stare off into space.

"Shit," Screech said at last.

"Well put," Beckett replied, finally looking over at the man. "Very succinct."

It had been a good two months since the day that Screech had come into Beckett's hospital room, handing him the note written by, then NYPD Sergeant, Chase Adams.

The one that had instructed him on what to say to Internal Affairs so that they wouldn't press charges for the murder of Craig Sloan.

Back then, Screech's hair had been unkempt and overgrown, like the head of a frayed Q-tip, and he sported a thin, wispy goatee. Now, the man's hair was closely cropped, almost shaved, and his goatee had grown out somewhat. He was still pale as ever and skinny as all hell, but Screech almost looked like a full-grown adult now.

"You never did tell me what you're doing here, Screech," Beckett said. "And while I'm grateful for a wingman, I get the sneaking suspicion that Drake might have had something to do with this."

Screech sipped his drink, a cocktail that looked as if it were powered by plutonium, before answering.

"No."

Beckett raised an eyebrow.

"No? Then Chase? Did Chase send you?"

"Wrong again."

"Really? I'm going to strike out twice in one day? Just tell me what you're doing here, bud."

Screech took his time and sipped away at his drink, which drove Beckett up the wall.

How does Drake deal with this guy?

"I'm here on business," Screech offered at last.

Beckett's eyebrows migrated up his forehead.

"Business? Since when did private investigators from New York come all the way to the Caribbean on 'business?' And how the hell did you and Drake afford a place like this?"

Screech shrugged.

"Triple D was commissioned to find a boat and Drake... well, he was otherwise occupied. Wait—not a boat. Drake gets pissed at me for calling it a boat. A *yacht*. A yacht named *B-yacht'ch*. Pretty hilarious if you ask me. Anyways, some guy lost his yacht and hired us to go find it for him."

Beckett ran a hand through his hair again, wondering if Screech was pulling his leg.

B-yacht'ch? Seriously?

If some rich asshole had actually named his yacht 'B-yacht'ch,' Beckett would have to give him props.

"How about you? How you holding up after—"

Beckett shook his head quickly, stemming the line of questioning before it gathered any steam.

"I'm fine," he lied, his eyes darting as he spoke. "That stuff with Craig? Craig Sloan? That was just a misunderstanding. A fucked-up, wrong place, wrong time, scenario—that's all. Don't know why everyone made such a big deal about it."

The truth was, however, Beckett *wasn't* fine, not really.

"But the rock... it was covered with—"

Beckett held up a hand.

"I'm fine," he repeated. "Just need a little R&R to get my mind off things."

Apparently satisfied, at least for the time being, Screech nodded and took another sip of his enriched plutonium. Beckett drained the rest of his rum, then signaled to the bartender that he needed a refill. As the bar's only two remaining patrons, the man was at their table, bottle in hand, in just a few short seconds.

"You know who that girl was?" the bartender asked, hooking a chin in the direction that Chloe had left.

"Yeah—her name's Chloe," Beckett said as he took a gulp of his newly filled drink.

The bartender tilted his head to one side.

"No, not her name—I never caught her name. But who she's *with*," he paused for effect. "She's with *Donnie*."

Beckett frowned.

"Yeah, she said that. She also said that she was a model and that she was here with Donnie to take some pictures and whatnot. Has some friends along for the ride. To be honest, it wasn't really her conversation skills that drew me to her."

The bartender hesitated and Beckett felt his frustration mount.

"Yes? And? T-t-t-today, junior."

The bartender's eyes, which had clouded over, cleared and he shook his head.

"Do you have any idea who Donnie is?"

Beckett looked at Screech and then both of them shrugged.

"Yeah, I can see that you two don't spend much time here in the islands. My advice? Stay away from her or anyone else involved with Donnie."

An image of Chloe in her string bikini as she walked away from the table flashed in Beckett's mind.

"I'll take that into consideration, weigh it with the positives," he said. "Anything else I can do for you?"

The bartender frowned.

"That's it," he said, making his way back to the bar. "I'd just stay away from her, is all. Just some friendly advice."

Yeah, Beckett thought. *You said that already—probably because you want to keep her all to yourself.*

And yet, in the back of his mind, the nagging words of the Internal Affairs goombas echoed.

Stay out of trouble, Beckett. Keep your head low for a while until this whole Craig Sloan thing blows over.

It was sage advice. Only problem was, Beckett always did have a problem listening and playing well with others.

Chapter 3

"I'LL TELL YOU WHAT, Screech," Beckett began. "You help me with Chloe and her friends, and I'll help you find your B-Yacht'ch."

Screech shook the empty glass in his hand and pressed his lips defiantly.

"What? What the hell does that mean?" Beckett demanded.

Screech rattled the ice in his glass again and Beckett finally figured out what the other man wanted. He rolled his eyes and shook his head but reached out and took Screech's glass from his hand and made his way over to the bar. Beckett didn't really need Screech—he knew from the moment that he'd told Chloe that he was a doctor that the deal was pretty much sealed. In his experience, there really was no better panty dropper than being a doctor. He wasn't sure why that was, but if he had to guess, it likely had some evolutionary roots in the ability to protect or heal or… something like that.

If only they knew I spend most of my days elbow deep in corpse entrails.

Beckett could imagine how a conversation at a bar much like this one might proceed should he be so brazenly honest.

Oh, so you're a doctor?

Yep.

Panties off

So, what do you do all day?

Oh, you know, cut people open, root around in their organs. Try to find out what rare and horrible disease killed them.

Chastity belt on

That's nice. I have to go now.

Wait—I haven't told you about the gunshot victims! People who are burned alive! Infanticide! Choking, drowning, stabbings!

Beckett shook his head.

Who am I kidding? They're just in it for the money.

He waved at the bartender, trying to get his attention. The truth was, while Beckett might not *need* Screech, he didn't feel like being alone right now, either.

The bartender made his way over, a smile on his face.

"What's your name?" he asked, realizing that despite their previous interactions, he still didn't know what to call the man. *Bartender* felt too informal, given how much time Beckett expected to spend in his presence over the next week or so.

"Kevin," the bartender offered, taking the two glasses from Beckett.

"Well, nice to meet you, Kevin. I'm Beckett. And that there—" he pointed to Screech who was staring at the sea, his back to them, "—is Screech."

"Pleasure to meet you guys," Kevin said, pouring Beckett more rum. "Does he want a refill, too?"

"Yeah, get him one of those plutonium drinks. Let's get him right fucked—maybe then he'll be less annoying."

The bartender chuckled, and as he turned to prep the drink, Beckett's attention remained focused on Screech.

The story of the search for a missing yacht, especially one with a name as unique and absurd as *B-Yacht'ch*, was too ridiculous to be made up, and yet Beckett still wasn't convinced that at least part of the reason Screech was here was to keep his eye on him.

And that meant that Drake thought he still wasn't right after what had happened.

I'm fine, he thought. *What'd I tell Screech? R&R. That's all I need—R&R.*

The bartender returned with the drinks and Beckett slipped a twenty from his shorts and laid it on the bar. Kevin looked at the bill for a moment, and Beckett, thinking that maybe this was a European thing in which tips were an insult, put his hand on it and was tempted to pull it back.

"What? Tips not allowed?"

"No," Kevin said. "They're allowed, but if you give me a twenty for every drink or two I make, you're going to go home broke."

Beckett shrugged.

"Fine. Not a tip then. Consider it a... *reward*."

Now it was Kevin's turn to raise an eyebrow.

"A reward? For what?"

Beckett smiled.

"For introducing me to the young lady, Chloe," Beckett tapped his temple. "For getting me laid, Kevin. That's what for. C'mon now."

Kevin's face suddenly changed.

"I didn't introduce you and I told you —"

Beckett rolled his eyes.

He didn't like *this* Kevin; he liked the *other* Kevin. The one that wasn't afraid of a little friendly, good-natured banter.

This Kevin was nearly as annoying as Screech.

"Yeah, yeah, yeah, you told me, Donnie Brasco, or whatever."

Beckett had meant the comment as a joke, an attempt to steer their conversation back into less serious waters, but Kevin was having none of it. The man's eyes, previously bright and wide in the afternoon sun, were suddenly two piss holes in the snow.

"Beckett," the man began in a low voice, casting a furtive glance around the bar to make sure that no one else was within earshot. "Donnie DiMarco is no joke. Look, I really think you should —"

Kevin was quickly killing his buzz.

"I'll tell you what," Beckett said, taking the drinks and stepping away from the bar. "Why don't we just let Chloe decide who she wants to sleep with? Hmm? That seems like the thing to do in this day and age, wouldn't you agree?"

Before Kevin could reply, Beckett turned his back on the bartender and walked over to Screech.

"You find your boat yet?"

Screech shook his head and took his drink from Beckett.

"No, not yet," he replied. Beckett was mildly aware of the fact that his own words were slightly slurred, but Screech? The man had seemingly lost the subtle art of including spaces in his sentences.

Ah, fuck it. I'm on vacation, after all. And so is he.

Beckett clinked glasses with Screech.

"Cheers," he said.

Screech paused for a moment, a confused expression on his face.

"What? What the fuck did I do now?"

"Cheers… do you know why we cheers?"

Beckett shrugged.

"An excuse to drink big gulps?"

Screech shook his head.

"No… it's from a long time ago when powerful families would try to settle their differences by marrying a son from one family with the daughter from another."

Beckett had to concentrate hard to make out what 'Spaceless' Screech was saying.

"And?"

"And they're all worried that the other family was going to poison their drinks. So, they would 'cheers' and swap some of the liquid in their glass with the other family, just to make sure it was safe to drink."

Beckett let this sink in for a moment.

"Wow. Fucking cheery lot at this resort," he said at last. "Listen, I'm not drinking any of your diabetic cocktail, I'll tell you that much. And the only person I want to swap fluids with is Chloe, so keep your half-chub in your shorts, cowboy."

Screech chuckled and turned his attention back to the ocean. Beckett followed the man's gaze and brought his glass of rum to his lips. Just before swallowing, however, he cast a glance over his shoulder to the bar.

Kevin was gone, but the twenty-dollar bill still flapped in the wind.

Fuck it, he thought with a shrug and then swallowed the rest of his rum in one gulp. *I'm going to have a good time despite everyone trying to bring me down.*

Chapter 4

THE ALCOHOL HIT SCREECH hard. It had been a tumultuous few weeks, and the level of stress he'd experienced was not in line with what he expected when taking the job as a computer analyst for a private investigation firm. Especially not one run by an ex-NYPD detective.

Of course, he never really had any interest in taking the job in the first place. No, Screech was quite happy toiling along making apps that generated just enough income to scrape by.

It was his stupid fucking brother. Three years his elder, but with less than half of his maturity, Larry Thompson could not, for the *worthless* life of him, stay out of trouble. And when it came to drug offenses, the District Attorney was not just open but *eager* to make a deal, to move up the chain of command, so to speak.

Provided you had something to offer in return, that is.

And Larry Thompson only had the shirt on his back, a filthy sweat-stained T-shirt, no less, to his name.

No dice, no deal.

Given his brother's past, Screech hadn't been surprised to get a call informing him of Larry's newest transgression. What had caught him off guard, however, was the DA implying with all the subtlety of an elephant hopped up on PCP that Screech might be able to help.

Me? What can I do?

The proposition had been as bizarre as it was confusing: interview for a very specific job and get it.

That job had been as a computer analyst with Triple D Investigations.

Screech had been skeptical but had had little choice in the matter. Besides, steady income never hurt anyone, did it?

But one thing Screech wasn't, was naive, and when shortly after getting the job an impish man who only went by 'Raul' came knocking, he knew that getting the job was only the first act in a much larger play.

Yet, never in his wildest dreams did Screech imagine that taking the job would have led him here: to a semiprivate island in the Caribbean, sipping cocktails in the warm afternoon sun.

Never in his wildest dreams did he imagine that he would become so involved in murder and death and everything else that seemed to follow Damien Drake around like a plague.

And the worst part? The worst part was that he really liked the man. Sure, Drake could do with an injection of humor, a heavy dose of jocularity, perhaps, but they had a pretty good Bonnie and Clyde routine going on.

He liked Beckett enough, too. In fact, before all of this shit had gone down, Screech had, for once in his life, found that he fit in, in a strange sort of way.

He felt like he belonged.

But after witnessing what Beckett had done to Craig Sloan...

A shudder coursed through Screech and he took a sip of his syrupy cocktail.

He should have never followed Drake and Beckett to the burning building.

He should have never snapped those photographs of Beckett with the bloody rock clutched in tensed fingers.

As haunting as those images were, Screech thought that he could overlook them all, chalk the event up to adrenaline and sheer emotion from what they had all been through at the hands of a demented ex-pathology resident.

But no matter how hard he tried to forget, something had lodged in Screech's brain, a parasite that simply refused to relinquish its deadly hold.

Beckett's eyes.

Screech had seen Beckett's eyes, and the vacuity therein — sheer and utter blankness after committing the worst act a human could — terrified him.

Just focus on the job, he chided himself as he stared out over the great expanse that was the North Atlantic Ocean. *Find the damn* B-Yacht'ch *first, then go from there. One step at a time.*

Screech took another sip of his drink and then rubbed his eyes. It was only midafternoon, but to him, it felt like midnight.

"Go get some rest," Beckett said, startling Screech out of his head. He had completely forgotten that the man was standing beside him.

"Wwwwha'?"

"I said, go get some sleep," Beckett repeated. "I need you as my wingman tonight."

The last thing Screech felt like doing was partying, especially given the ominous warning from the bartender, but it didn't look like he was going to get out of this one.

Roped in again...

"Alrrrrright," he said reluctantly, setting his half-finished drink down on an empty table. "Wwwhat *djyou* think 'bout meeting for dinner 'round sssseven?"

Beckett slapped him on the back.

"That's more like it. Go get some rest, something tells me we're going to have one hell of a night."

Chapter 5

BECKETT'S ASSERTION THAT SCREECH should get some sleep was also self-serving: he too was run-down. He watched Screech stagger toward the main reception building, and when he was out of sight, Beckett made his way toward his villa.

The interior of the hexagonal, wood and straw villa was musty smelling, and the first thing Beckett did after entering was open the large window above the kitchenette. Taking a deep breath of the briny air, he closed his eyes and allowed the afternoon sun to wash over his face.

Beckett stayed this way for several moments before his hand slipped on the counter and he realized that he must have dozed off.

Get some rest, Beckett. Recharge for tonight, he instructed himself.

The villa itself was designed to sleep six—or twelve, depending on #sharing—and Beckett decided that he would sleep in a new bed every night.

Hopefully with a new companion, as well. A new companion sporting a string bikini that could double as dental floss.

Hey, there's an idea...

But for now, he simply selected the nearest room and stepped inside.

Unlike the main entrance, the bedroom smelled clean and fresh. Arms splayed, he collapsed on the bed.

He was asleep in seconds.

***

"You killed her," Beckett hissed through clenched teeth.

The man dressed in the black tracksuit stared back at him, his eyes dark, his expression tense. He didn't say anything—he didn't have to.

Beckett did enough talking for the both of them.

"You killed all those people," he spat. "You killed my students."

His fingers tensed on the palm-sized stone in his hand and, without thinking, Beckett took a large step forward.

This time, the man did move. Only he didn't turn to run as Beckett suspected he might; instead, he simply lowered his eyes to the stone, then held his hands out to his sides.

"This was all just a game to you, wasn't it? A sick, twisted game to get back at a teacher who scorned you... and you think that that gives you the right to kill?"

The man's thin lips twisted into a sneer and he started to raise the pistol in his right hand.

"You don't understand..."

Beckett took another step forward, closing the distance between them.

"Oh, I understand all right. What I understand is —"

Craig Sloan's finger tightened on the trigger, but just as Beckett suspected, the only sound that came from the barrel was a hollow click.

Beckett's smile grew.

"—what I understand," he continued, more slowly this time, "is that someone needs to stop you before you kill again. What I understand, is that you are the one who deserves to die."

Craig lowered the gun and Beckett saw his legs tense as if he were about to pounce, or worse, turn and run.

"And that person is you?" Craig said with a leer of his own. "Isn't that ironic. Who are you —"

Beckett lunged.

He was an athletic man, one who kept in shape, and yet Beckett couldn't remember a time in the last ten years that he had moved so quickly.

Like his victims, Craig Sloan had no chance.

The stone struck the man above his right eye, spraying Beckett's hand and arms with blood.

But Craig Sloan didn't go down; he staggered, but somehow managed to keep his footing.

Somewhere to his left, Beckett became aware of the roaring heat of the burning house, of the crackle of wood followed by the collapse of a large section of the roof.

But he paid this little heed; he only had one job to do now.

Beckett had to stop this murderer before he struck again.

As Craig struggled to collect his bearings, Beckett reared back and smashed the stone against his head again, this time striking him in the temple.

Craig's eyes rolled back in his head and he collapsed awkwardly, his shoulder ricocheting off the house to his right before his face smashed on the flagstones.

A dark pool that looked like an oil slick in the moonlight immediately started to form around Craig's nose and mouth.

Beckett tilted his head to one side, observing the fallen man for a moment before his arm suddenly went slack and he lowered the stone to his hip.

He was about to drop it; Beckett had every intention of letting the stone slip from his fingers and rushing to get Drake or Detective Adams. Or the ambulance, even; there were small bubbles forming in the pool of the man's own blood.

Craig was still breathing.

But as he stared at that blood, Beckett didn't see the reflection of moonlight. Instead, he saw Craig Sloan's victims. He saw Toby Teager, who Craig Sloan had electrocuted, and then Jane Doe who had been drowned in Central Park. He saw Martin Dean, whose wrists had been slit, and Gerald Leblanc, who had been shot in the head. And he also saw Dr. Eddie Larringer, his own student, who Craig had hung and made to look like a suicide.

But the one person who put Beckett over the edge was Suzan. Suzan Cuthbert's face, her tongue poking into her cheek as she scribbled furiously, trying to finish the pathology exam ahead of the other students, was so real that, for an instant, Beckett thought that she was actually there.

Except Craig had tied Suzan up in the house to his right that was slowly being reduced to embers.

Instead of dropping the stone, Beckett tightened his grip.

And then he swung it again.

And again.

And again.

Beckett kept smashing the stone against Craig's head until he was soaked with blood and his arm was so tired that he couldn't even raise it to wipe the sweat from his brow.

Chapter 6

SCREECH KEPT HIS HEAD low as he made his way towards the main lobby. Unlike Beckett, he didn't have the funds nor the connections for his own villa. Even with Bob Bumacher's rather generous stipend, Screech was only able to afford a small apartment situated above the main reception area, which he assumed was occupied by staff during the high season. He shuffled past the reception desk, not wanting to make eye contact with the concierge who seemed to take great pride in not only being the most cheerful person on the island but quite possibly on planet Earth, as well.

Screech, on the other hand, didn't feel so jovial at the moment.

Thankfully, the elevator was waiting on the ground floor, and it took a grand total of six seconds to rise one story — the ride was so short, in fact, that it made Screech think of the half floors in the movie *Being John Malkovich*. He didn't know about becoming John, but Screech might not have turned down the opportunity to slide inside someone else's skin if only for a little while. Just until he forgot about Craig Sloan.

Screech shook his head as he made his way down the short hallway to his room, scrounging in his pockets for his keycard as he walked.

He didn't find it.

"Shit," he muttered under his breath. A quick search of all his pockets, including the one on his shirt, came up empty.

With a sigh, Screech tried to think back to where he might've left the key. He had it when he left the room — he was *pretty* sure he had it when he left the room — but things got muddy after his first drink, and downright opaque after the third.

"Where the hell are you?"

Out of options, Screech resigned himself to going back to the front desk to talk to Captain Cheerful to get a replacement.

He was partway to the elevator when his phone buzzed. He hadn't lost that, at least. Part of him hoped that it was Drake calling to check in with him, if nothing else but to show that he gave a shit.

But the message wasn't from Drake; it was from Bob Bumacher.

Any updates? Remember to be discreet.

Screech raised an eyebrow and considered writing back with something 'discreet'... like a dick pic. After only a second of half-serious contemplation, he slid the phone back into his pocket without responding. Whenever he had a few drinks, Screech tended to make stupid—*stupider*—decisions. And while he knew little of the giant bald man with the cartoon name—Bob Bumacher—he had quickly learned that the man had the same sense of humor as a plum. And as Drake, for that matter.

Time sluiced forward as it tended to do when one imbibed, and Screech eventually found himself back in the lobby. He raised his eyes to the reception desk, a fake smile plastered on his face for the benefit of Captain Cheerful.

Only the concierge wasn't alone and he no longer looked cheerful.

"What? I don't care. I told you that I want Kevin to bartend on my boat. No one else; *just Kevin*," a man with a thick, black beard and closely cropped hair said. Screech didn't need to see the two bikini-clad women, a blond on one arm, a brunette on the other, to know who this man was. It was in the way he spoke, with such authority and unwavering confidence, that gave it away.

The concierge's lips twisted into a frown, immediately attempted to rise in a smile, but fell just short. In the end, Captain Cheerful settled on a neutral expression.

"I'm sorry, Mr. DiMarco. I really am. But the rules are—"

Donnie DiMarco reached into his swim trunks and pulled out a rolled-up wad of bills that he promptly slapped on the desk.

"What rules are these?"

Captain Cheerful's eyes flicked to the bills before rising again to Donnie's face. He was smiling again; they both were.

"I truly am sorry, Mr. DiMarco. But this isn't a matter of funding. It's about the license, about the—"

When Donnie reached across the table and grabbed the concierge by the collar, Screech gasped. The sound confused him, as he was fairly certain that only preteens gasped in the presence of their favorite boy band, and at first, he didn't think that it had come from his mouth.

But when all eyes—the concierge, Donnie, the two models—turned on him, he was positive that he had.

Screech reached for the elevator close button, but he missed it and instead pressed the red emergency button. A loud chime went off and he cringed.

"Fuck me," he grumbled under his breath.

Donnie DiMarco let go of the concierge and then wrapped his arms around his ladies protectively.

"Carlos, Carlos, Carlos, you shyster, you. You said we were the only ones here," Donnie said with a grin.

Screech couldn't tell if the man was hitting on Carlos or was about to execute a hit on him. Either way, it was all very confusing.

What in the Christ was in those drinks?

"No, sir, I never said that you were—"

Donnie waved a hand dismissively and Carlos went quiet.

"What's your name, son?"

With the elevator alarm still going off, Screech could barely make out the man's words. He fumbled for the alarm button.

"What?" he shouted.

Eventually, his fingers found it and the chime silenced.

"What did you—" Screech's words were so loud now that his ears started to ring. He lowered his voice. "Pardon? What did you say?"

Donnie DiMarco chuckled. He had a pleasant face beneath the thick beard and striking blue eyes.

"Got into the sauce a little early, didn't you?"

Screech swallowed hard, tasting the cloying remnants of every molecule ending in *-ose*—glucose, fructose, sucrose... lactose? Yeah, there was probably lactose in there as well— that had been used to sweeten his cocktails.

"Yeah, I guess."

"Well, kid, I asked for your name."

"Screech," he replied quickly.

Although his attention was focused on Donnie, he couldn't help but sweep his eyes to the beauties under each of the man's arms. Chloe, the woman from the bar, had been undeniably beautiful. But these girls... they were *tens*.

No, *elevens—hundreds. Millions.* Christ, he had never seen women this hot before.

"Screech? Like, *Saved by the Bell*? That Screech?"

Screech nodded and was going to add something else when the elevator chirped at him again. Startled, he stepped into the lobby and the doors closed behind him.

"Hey, hey, hey, what's going on here?" Donnie said with a smile, removing his hand from the oiled back of the blond and extending it. "Just fucking with you. I'm Donnie."

Screech reached for the man's hand. He never had a firm handshake and was of the mind that a man with a hard handshake was making up for something else that was just a little too soft. But Donnie's grip... it wasn't hard. It was like a *vice*. And when Screech tried to pull his hand back, Donnie didn't let him. At least, not at first.

"So, tell me, Screech, what are you doing tonight?"

Screech's first instinct was to tell Donnie about his plan to meet up with Beckett, and maybe Chloe, for dinner but changed his mind at the last second.

"Nothing," he said with a shrug and Donnie finally let go of his hand. "Just watching the sunset, I guess."

Donnie's blue eyes bored into him, and for a brief moment, Screech thought that the man would read through his lie. But then his mouth parted in the perfect grin.

"Well, I'll tell you what, Screech. Why don't you come visit my yacht tonight; you can watch the sunset from there." Donnie cast a glance to the girls under his arms. "And anything else you might want to feast your eyes on."

Screech couldn't help but smirk.

"Sounds like I just might join you, Donnie," he said. "Where's the yacht... parked?"

"It's the only one on the island — *moored* on the North Dock. It should be a good time... especially given that we will have the best bartender in all of the Virgin Gorda serving us drinks. Isn't that right, Carlos?" Donnie cast a glance at the bills that were still on the desk in front of the concierge. "Anyways, you can't miss it. The yacht is called *'B-Yacht'ch'*. So don't you be one and forget to show up, Screech. Oh, and if your pals AC Slater or Zach Morris are around, let them know that all of Bayside is invited."

Chapter 7

BECKETT AWOKE WITH A scream caught in his throat. He sat bolt upright on his bed, but his skin was so clammy that his sheets clung to him and almost pulled him back down. It took him a moment to realize where he was, and nearly a minute to draw a full breath.

Craig's gone... there's nothing you can do about it now.

Despite being drenched in sweat, when Beckett tried to swallow, he was unable; his mouth and throat were incredibly dry. With a groan, he rolled off the bed and made his way to the bathroom. Once there, he splashed frigid water on his face, hoping that it would shock the nightmare from his mind.

When that didn't work, he simply held his face directly under the tap.

After the numbing effect took hold, Beckett raised his head and caught sight of his reflection in the mirror. His eyes were red-rimmed and his face was paler than it normally was despite the sun he'd gotten that afternoon. He brushed some of the water from his bleach-blond hair and then stood up tall, forcing his lungs to inflate to their capacity. His chest was covered with tattoos, starting from just below his collarbone and running down most of his abdomen. On his left pec, he had a black-and-white photorealistic tattoo of a bull's head, while his right was adorned with a Celtic symbol that meant 'warrior.' He had sparrows on each of his shoulders, their dark beaks aimed downward at cherry blossoms on one triceps and a feathered quill passing through the center of an ouroboros on the other. All of these tattoos, and the many others that filled the space between the major works of art held a special meaning to him. And yet one of these was more important than the others. *Far* more important.

Becket lifted his right arm and stared at the three-inch vertical line that ran across his ribs directly beneath where his armpit hair ended.

He stared at that eighth of an inch thick line for several moments before realizing that he was holding his breath. It was the simplest of all of his tattoos and the only one that he'd done himself.

"Craig Sloan," Beckett whispered as he ran his index finger along the length of the line.

Craig had been a bad man, and he'd done bad things. Beckett had put an end to that. And now Craig would be with him forever.

Beckett shuddered then dried himself completely. After applying some paste to his hair, he made his way back to the suitcase that hung open at the foot of his bed. He slid on a pair of faded blue jean shorts and a graphic T-shirt emblazoned with the band Korn across the chest.

Then, after a deep, sighing breath, he shook away the vestigial cobwebs of his nightmare and pulled the door to his villa wide.

And then he nearly bowled Screech over.

"Fuck," Beckett cried, stumbling back into his villa. "Screech? What the hell are you doing here?"

The man's face was pale and his lips were cream-colored.

"Screech?" Beckett asked again, his concern mounting. He reached out and laid a hand on the man's shoulder and a tremor passed through both of them. Beckett pulled Screech into his villa and closed the door behind them. "What the hell happened to you? What's going on?"

Screech swallowed hard and then licked his lips before answering.

"It's Donnie..." he said in a quiet voice.

Beckett raised an eyebrow and observed Screech for a moment before commenting. The man was still wearing exactly what he had been at the bar and, judging by the smell of alcohol on his breath, he hadn't bothered showering or napping.

"Donnie? You mean the guy that Chloe was talking about? The guy who's having the party on his boat tonight?"

Beckett was having a hard time coming to grips with what exactly was going on, what had happened to his friend.

"I met him... Donnie DiMarco."

Beckett's eyes flicked side to side. He felt as if he'd missed the punchline of a joke and everyone else was laughing.

"And? Did he touch you or something? Did he diddle—"

Screech shook his head.

"No, he was with these girls... these beautiful girls," Screech paused and leveled his eyes at Beckett. "It's *his* yacht. *His* yacht is called *B-Yacht'ch*."

Again, Beckett was at a loss.

"I have no clue what you're talking about, Screech. I don't know if our friendly neighborhood bartender put something in your—"

"No, Beckett, it's not that. It's the yacht... it's Donnie DiMarco's yacht... he called it *B-yacht'ch*. It's the yacht that I came here looking for."

Chapter 8

"THIS SEEMS... DOWNRIGHT RETARDED," Screech said, scratching his goatee.

Beckett shrugged.

"You got any better ideas?"

"Just about any idea is better than this one," Screech replied.

Beckett rolled his eyes.

"I don't know why you're acting so fucking weird... I mean, you came here looking for the yacht and now you found it. You should be happy. *Ka-ching*, am I right?"

Screech frowned.

"Why don't we just call the cops?"

Beckett took a sip of the scotch in his hand and looked around before answering. The sun had started to set and the two men found themselves back at the same outdoor bar as earlier in the day. Just a few hours ago, in fact. Only this time, Kevin had been replaced by a balding fifty-something-year-old bartender who poured light drinks in glasses stained with only god knows what.

"Yeah? You ever dealt with Caribbean cops before?"

Screech, who was gulping a glass of seltzer water, narrowed his eyes at him.

"No," he spat. "Have you?"

Beckett shook his head.

"No—but still. Anyways, you know what happened in..." an image of the rock covered in blood and bone and brain matter flashed in Beckett's mind and he shuddered. "...New York. I'm on double-secret probation here, Screech. I can't be getting involved with the cops."

Screech took an annoyingly long sip of his water.

"So, you think that instead of getting the cops involved, it's a better idea to board a mob boss's yacht, snap pictures of him and the vessel, then blackmail him into giving the yacht back? That pretty much sums up your plan?"

Beckett had to admit that Screech had a point—it wasn't the most genius of plans. But his skinny friend forgot the most important part: Chloe.

He *had* to see Chloe again. And besides, a party was exactly what Beckett needed to take his mind off things. It likely wasn't what Internal Affairs had in mind when they'd suggested a vacation but fuck it.

Those pencil pushers weren't here now, were they?

"Look, the guy invited us. And based on how you described him, I bet taking pictures would flatter Donnie. Anyways, we'll just snap the pics and send them to Bob Bumhugger or whatever the fuck his name is and go from there. If things get really hairy, we'll call Drake. How does *that* sound?"

Screech chewed the inside of his lip.

"Aren't you a partner at Triple D, anyway?" Beckett needled. "Do you think Drake would have sent you here if he didn't think that you could handle the job?"

Screech scowled and took the bait.

"Fine, we'll do it your way. We'll go to the party and snap pictures. But if things get fucked-up... I'm not—I'm not—"

"You're not what? Jesus, spit it out already."

Screech finished his seltzer water in one gulp.

"Nothing," he said, lowering his gaze. "Can you promise me one thing, at least?"

Beckett sipped his scotch.

"I'm not kissing you, man."

Screech ignored the comment.

"Just don't get fucking drunk off your ass, okay?"

Beckett finished his scotch in three swallows.

"Me? Never."

***

It was clear from the moment that they saw the yacht that it was the one that Screech was looking for. Even if the word 'B-Yacht'ch' wasn't boldly emblazoned on the back, the tinted windows, the gold handrails, the loud music, and flashing lights all screamed that the owner was... well, a *biatch*. As Screech and Beckett approached the loading platform, they were greeted by human refrigerators crammed into matching black suits, their arms crossed over their chests. It was all so cliché that Beckett couldn't help but smirk.

"Gentlemen," he exclaimed as Screech slid in behind him.

The man on the left took one look at Beckett's spiky blond hair, his worn jeans, and T-shirt, and frowned.

"Private party," he said simply.

"Oh, you can speak," Beckett said under his breath. "Nice trick."

"What was that?" the bouncer on the right demanded.

"Nothing. It's just that if you check your guest list there, you'll see that we were invited," Beckett said.

"By who?" the men asked in unison.

"The Dalai Lama. Who the fuck do you think?"

The man on the right unfolded his massive arms and looked about to move forward when Screech spoke up.

"Yeah, you don't look like his type. Why don't—"

The bouncer stopped speaking when the man himself appeared, needing no introduction. Sporting a silk robe that hung open revealing a pair of short, swim trunks beneath,

Beckett knew that this was Donnie the way he knew that the yacht was *B-yacht'ch*. But Beckett was far more interested in the woman at his side, than the man himself.

It was Chloe.

"Hey, Screech!" Donnie shouted with a wave. The bouncers turned and then quickly parted to allow Screech and Beckett to pass.

"You guys are cute, you know that?" Beckett whispered as he strutted by the men. "Like Bobbsey Twins born in Chernobyl."

Screech hurried up to the main deck and this time it was Beckett's turn to follow.

"Nice to see you again," Donnie said, offering Screech a strong handshake. "This your boy AC or Zach?"

Although Beckett got the reference, he frowned in disapproval.

Lame.

"The name's Beckett."

Donnie made an O shape with his mouth.

"Well, nice to meet you, Beckett. My name's Donnie, and this is my yacht. You guys want a drink?"

Before either of them could answer, Donnie nodded vigorously and then released his hold on Chloe.

"Of course, you do. Chloe, sweetheart, want to grab some drinks for our guests?"

Chloe nodded, her head kept low, and then started toward the front of the yacht.

"I'll go with you," Beckett offered quickly.

This time, it was he who didn't wait for an answer.

Chapter 9

"YOU SHOULDN'T BE HERE," Chloe whispered.

Beckett hurried to catch up with the woman, his brow furrowed.

"I'm sorry, m'lady, but I'm getting mixed messages. Didn't you just invite me a few hours ago?"

Chloe ducked behind a pillar supporting a staircase and then grabbed Beckett roughly by the shoulders.

"I'm no prude, but perhaps you should buy me a drink first," Beckett said with a grin.

But Chloe wasn't smiling.

"Beckett, you need to get out of here. Things have... things have changed. Donnie isn't... he isn't who I thought he was."

The alarm in her voice and the fear on her face gave Beckett pause. He glanced around quickly to catch his bearings. They were alone by the staircase, but everywhere else on the boat seemed to be populated by beautiful women. Normally, he would have considered this a blessing, but there was something that didn't fit. Beckett counted at least two dozen women, all beautiful, all scantily clad in bikinis, but it was what he *didn't* see that was odd.

Aside from himself, Donnie, Screech, the bartender, Kevin, and the two goons by the boarding ramp, there were no other men on board.

Gives me good odds, Beckett thought. And he would have said as much, if Chloe hadn't looked so damn scared.

"What's going on, Chloe? Is he... is he hitting you?" Beckett asked, his eyes narrowing.

There was something else odd about the scene, he realized as he watched Chloe's face undergo several different emotions in rapid succession. All the women on the boat, save Chloe, were drinking from coconuts that Kevin was hacking away at off to one side.

"I found other women," Chloe said softly. "On the boat."

Beckett raised an eyebrow and looked around again.

"Umm… yeah, plenty of women here. In fact —"

Chloe leaned in close and pinched Beckett's arm.

"No, not here… *below*. They're below deck and they are —"

A smiling Donnie DiMarco suddenly appeared from around the corner and Chloe immediately let go of Beckett's arm.

A smile effortlessly slid onto her face, but it took Beckett considerably more effort to match the expression.

"That's where you went," Donnie said. "The bar's over there. You're not trying to pull one on with my woman, are you, good doctor?"

Beckett chuckled and held up his hands defensively.

"No such thing. In fact, I was trying to stave off her advances."

Donnie reached out and gave Chloe's ass a light slap.

"Yeah, she's all about the new guys. Go on, sweetie, go find your sister."

Beckett's eyebrows rose at the mention of a sister.

"Now, about that drink, Beckett? You still interested?"

Beckett nodded and together they walked over to the bartender.

Kevin raised his head. When he locked eyes with Beckett, his lip curled ever so slightly.

"What can I get you, Donnie?" the man asked.

Beckett still couldn't figure out what Kevin's deal was, but considering Chloe's clandestine comment, he was no longer convinced that it had entirely to do with keeping the girls to himself.

Some of them, certainly, but even a guy as young as Kevin would have a hard time satisfying all the women.

And, besides, sharing was caring.

"I'm gonna guess that the good doctor is a Scotch man. Let's hook him up with some of the good stuff."

Beckett's eyes fell on the five or six coconuts that Kevin had been working on.

"What? No umbrella coconut drink for you?" he asked.

Donnie's smile faltered, but only for a second.

"No," the man replied. "Those are for the ladies."

How chivalrous of you, Beckett thought. *How chivalrous for a man keeping ladies below deck.*

Chapter 10

THERE'S SOMETHING WRONG HERE, Screech thought.

It was in the way that the women holding coconuts swayed to the music, the way their eyes were glassy, that tipped him off.

There was something else, too, something that he couldn't quite place. Screech wasn't sure if this wasn't just his paranoia rearing its ugly head, or if Drake's detective instincts were somehow rubbing off on him.

Whatever it was, he simply couldn't shake the feeling.

I need to get out of here, he thought. *I need to take some pictures, confirm that this is the boat, then call Bob Bumacher.*

The good news was that with the women acting the way they were, they didn't notice him slip away from the main deck. A furtive glance at the goons guarding the ramp showed that they were also preoccupied. And yet, based only on his brief encounter with Donnie DiMarco, he didn't doubt that the man had other people, those less easy to identify, making sure that nothing got out of hand.

After all, no one steals a two- or three-million-dollar yacht and doesn't expect some sort of retribution.

Screech took a seat on the cushions near the stern and marveled at how comfortable the seat was. It was as if everything on this yacht was made of clouds, and the women were floating on them.

It made him wonder how a man like Bob could 'lose' the yacht in the first place. As his eyes drifted upward, he saw dozens of whirling electronics and swaying antennae on the roof of the second level.

Bob couldn't track the behemoth by GPS? Surely a ship as large as this would be easy to track... why did he come to us?

Screech shook his head and lowered his eyes. He could see Chloe speaking to one of her other bikini-clad friends, the latter of which was taking heavy pulls on the thick straw jutting from her coconut. Chloe seemed agitated and upset and tried to swat the drink from the other woman's hands, but the woman, who appeared intoxicated, stumbled away from her. The commotion had started to draw the attention of others, and Screech used this distraction to his advantage.

With a final glance at the men in the black suits by the ramp, he turned and flipped over the railing. He landed on a platform a few inches from the water and then pressed his back against the rear of the boat.

When no one shouted and he heard nobody running in his direction, Screech exhaled a sigh of relief. Then, gathering his wits once more, he shifted his position so that he could take a good look at the writing on the back of the yacht.

"*B-yacht'ch*, British Virgin Islands," Screech read under his breath as he pulled his cell out of his pocket. He snapped a few pictures, making sure that they clearly showed the name in the low lighting, then scrolled to Bob Bumacher's contact. A moment before he clicked send, however, a thought occurred to him.

It came out of nowhere, but as soon as it had, he wondered why he hadn't thought of it sooner: *What if this isn't Bob's yacht?*

When the huge, bald man had come to Triple D and asked them to find his yacht, Screech had been green under the gills. But that had been before... before what had happened with Beckett and Craig Sloan. At the time, Screech had been eager to accept the case, to branch out from following octogenarians around to ensure that the help didn't steal their silverware, and also to show his partner Drake that he could handle something like this.

But now he was second-guessing his initial judgment.

Who's to say that this is actually Bob's yacht?

After all, he'd never provided a single shred of evidence that it was, and Screech hadn't thought to ask. And as far as he knew, Bob had never gone to the police. Even stranger was the fact that the man had only wanted them to find the boat, not retrieve it.

The job was to locate the boat and let Bob know of the location—that was it.

As this idea took up precedence in his mind, Screech thought back to Donnie's casual demeanor in the resort lobby. Sure, the man was being a dick, but he didn't seem in the least concerned of being found out. And the name... surely, a man who'd just stolen a three-million-dollar yacht would try to disguise a name as unique as *B-yacht'ch*, wouldn't he?

Just staring at those letters now, Screech thought that with just a few pieces of electrical tape, he could change the name to something less conspicuous.

Screech's finger continued to hover over the send button as he tried to figure out what to do next.

Should I call Drake? Ask his opinion?

He shook his head.

No, this is my case. I can do this. I'm a partner now, I need to start acting like one.

A shout drew him out of his head, and Screech carefully peered around the side of the yacht.

Two tanned men in fatigues sporting automatic weapons over their shoulders chatted as they made their way toward the yacht.

Screech swallowed hard.

Maybe the police had been notified after all—or the local militia or whatever governing body oversaw this part of the world.

Either way, Screech knew that it would be in his best interests to get off the majestic vessel as soon as possible.

If he valued his freedom, that is.

After a few deep breaths, Screech sent the images to Bob Bumacher, wondering the entire time how he'd gotten himself into this mess.

Chapter 11

THE BARTENDER KEPT SHOOTING eyes at Beckett as he poured his Scotch. Beckett did his best to ignore the man.

The Scotch he was served was indeed the 'good stuff.' Although Beckett never saw the bottle, he pegged it as a twenty-five or thirty-year-old Glenlivet.

"Damn good," Beckett said under his breath.

"Indeed," Donnie concurred, taking a sip of his own drink. Then he wrapped his arm around Beckett's shoulder, something that instantly made him uncomfortable. He wasn't sure what it was about Donnie that was off-putting, but it was more than just Kevin and Chloe's warnings.

It was the way in which everything the man said and did was friendly but wasn't. It was all... passive aggressive.

And yet, Beckett didn't shrink away from the man's grasp. They were of equal height, but Donnie had him by about twenty pounds. If push came to shove, Beckett suspected that he wouldn't be the one doing the shoving.

"Hey, Beckett, you want to go somewhere and chat?" Donnie asked as he led the man away from the bar and toward the front of the yacht.

Beckett looked around, noting a bunch of the girls congregating off to one side.

"Not really," he admitted. "I'd rather stay here with the ladies."

Donnie chuckled.

"Yeah, me too. But there's something I want to talk to you about."

Beckett raised an eyebrow.

And then, as he stared at Donnie DiMarco's bearded face, he realized something, something that had happened a few moments ago that he hadn't picked up on.

I'm gonna guess that the good doctor is a Scotch man. Let's hook him up with some of the good stuff, Donnie had said.

But Beckett hadn't mentioned that he was a doctor, not once. He supposed that Kevin might have told him, or maybe even Chloe, but something told him this wasn't the case.

Donnie already knew he was a doctor; Beckett was sure of it.

Kevin brought the machete down hard on the side of a coconut, sending a green shard over the side of the yacht.

"Well, okay," Beckett agreed. "Maybe then you can tell me how you knew I was a doctor because I think I rather look like a rock star than a man of medicine, myself."

Beckett tried to gauge the man's reaction to this, but Donnie's face remained stoic.

"What are the odds?" Donnie said with a smug expression that Beckett didn't care for. "I'm looking for a doctor to join my team."

Beckett's eyes narrowed.

In his experience, any 'team' that needed the service of a doctor that didn't wear jerseys with numbers on the back was never a good thing.

And given the reason behind why he was here on vacation—a "voluntary" suspension—Beckett knew better than to get into bed with Donnie DiMarco.

"On second thought, I think I'll pass. I'm in the—"

The commotion that had begun not twenty feet from them suddenly escalated to shouts and Beckett turned to see a red-faced Chloe on the verge of coming to blows with another bikini-clad woman.

Beckett moved in their direction, but Donnie stayed him with his hand and tilted his head toward the ramp leading up to the yacht.

It was then that Beckett noticed the two men with machine guns in the process of boarding.

Uh-oh, he thought. *This can't be good.*

His initial thought was that they were coming for him, that the NYPD had changed their mind and had decided that they would press charges against him after all. His second was that the man who'd hired Screech, Bob Bum-ache or whatever his name was, had called in reinforcements.

Either way, Beckett was confident that this wasn't a good place for him to be found.

Despite his inclination to go to Chloe, he decided instead to hang low and observe the situation. As he did, he noticed that many of the girls that had been above board a moment ago had since disappeared.

Did they go below *like Chloe had said? Were they... illegals, maybe? Was there such a thing as being an illegal alien on the Virgin Gorda?*

But before he could give this much thought, however, Beckett realized that someone else was also missing: Screech.

Where the fuck did he go?

Donnie suddenly left his side and walked over to the two men with automatic weapons. The man on the left, a thick fellow wearing a camo hat, switched his rifle from his back to his front and gripped the stock tightly in one hand.

This can't be good. No way can this be good.

Beckett cringed when Donnie reached out and laid a hand on one of the armed men's shoulders. He expected the hard-looking man with the grimace to swat Donnie's hand away, but he didn't. If anything, he leaned in closer. Then Donnie said something that Beckett couldn't make out. Without uttering a word to Donnie, the man clutching the stock of his weapon turned and whispered something in his partner's ear.

Then they both nodded and Donnie reached into a hidden pocket within his satin robe.

Just as he started to pull something out, a voice from behind drew Beckett's attention.

"Doctor? Beckett?"

Beckett turned around to stare at the bartender. Kevin's expression was grim, and Beckett noted that the man's hands—one holding a machete, the other half a coconut—were shaking badly.

"What?"

"You shouldn't be here," Kevin said. "You should get out of here while you still can—this isn't... it isn't what it seems."

Beckett rolled his eyes. This mantra, coming from both the bartender or Chloe, was starting to annoy him.

"All right, thanks, tips," he said. He was about to add more when someone's hand came down on his shoulder.

It was Donnie, and he was smiling again.

"Now, about that chat..."

Chapter 12

SCREECH DIDN'T SPEAK SPANISH if indeed that was what Donnie and the militia were speaking, but money was the universal language, and bribery was the ultimate manifestation.

As he watched, Donnie produced a thick envelope from beneath his silk robe and handed it to one of the men in fatigues. That was the extent of their interaction; the men promptly shifted their automatic weapons to their backs and left the yacht. This time, however, the bouncers guarding the ramp didn't bother moving out of the way and the militia were forced to squeeze past.

Next, Donnie dispelled whatever argument that Chloe was having with several of the other girls and returned to Beckett's side.

Screech's legs were starting to cramp and, satisfied with all that was going on and that he wasn't being observed, he hoisted himself over the railing. But even after he took a seat on the plush cushion as if he'd never left, his efforts to remain inconspicuous were foiled by his telephone beeping loudly in his pocket.

"Shit," he grumbled.

It was a message from Bob: *Where are you? Stay low, don't engage. Use discretion.*

Screech scowled.

Don't engage? I'm a fucking computer analyst, not some sort of covert ops agent.

He debated writing something to this effect but changed his mind at the last moment; Bob didn't strike him as someone who shared his unique sense of humor. Instead, he sent the resort address and instructed Bob to hurry.

Despite being inundated with beautiful women, there was a bad vibe on the yacht, something that Screech wanted no part of.

But before he could slink off, a brunette with shortly cropped hair and high cheekbones appeared out of nowhere. She sidled up next to him and started to massage his shoulders.

He instinctively shrugged her off.

"What's wrong, sweetie?" the woman asked. "You seem tense."

"Yeah, no shit."

"Well, maybe you just need a drink," she continued. Although her words were slurred, Screech detected an accent of sorts; Spanish, maybe.

The woman adjusted her position and in the process spilled some of her coconut drink on the cushion beside him.

"Whoopsie," she said with a lopsided grin.

The liquid smelled bitter and unappealing, leaving Screech to wonder how in the world she could actually drink the stuff.

"No thanks," he said. It was a lie; he wanted—no, he *needed* a drink—but first and foremost, he wanted off the yacht.

But before Screech could rise, another woman, a redhead with vibrant green eyes, took up residence on the other side of him.

She too seemed wobbly on her feet and clutched a coconut loosely in one hand.

"You sure you don't want a drink?" the redhead asked.

Screech shook his head.

"No, I've had enough. And I think you have, too."

The woman pouted and searched for the pink straw jutting from the coconut with her mouth. She chased it around for a few seconds until Screech became so unnerved that he grabbed it and put it to her lips.

With this new distraction, Screech managed to finagle his way out of the woman's grasp and hurried to the front of the yacht in search of Beckett.

Only Beckett was no longer there. He glanced around but saw no sign of the man; all he saw were more drunk bikini-clad women.

Screech turned to the bartender.

"Hey, did you see where Beckett went?" he asked.

Kevin had a solemn expression on his face, which served to put Screech further on edge.

"Beckett... did you see where he went?"

Kevin shrugged and shook his head.

"He was right here... you sure you didn't see where he went?"

The man's dark eyes darted about, and then indicated for Screech to lean forward.

"You should get out of here, Screech."

Screech frowned; the man was starting to sound like a broken record.

"Not without my friend. Did you see him or not?"

When Kevin didn't answer, Screech used all of his willpower not to reach across the makeshift bar and throttle the man. A quick glance at the two men in suits guarding the ramp quickly put a damper on these plans. With a grunt of frustration, Screech backed away from the bar and made his way around the staircase where he'd last seen Beckett. He looked upward first, but only saw another harem of women. That's where Beckett likely *wanted* to go, but something told him that this wasn't where Donnie had taken his friend. Screech's eyes drifted downward next.

He wanted to head into the dark underbelly of the yacht like he wanted to stick a hot needle into his eye.

But he was as loyal as he was frightened.

With another deep breath, Screech stepped onto the first rung of the staircase and started to descend.

What kind of mess have you gotten yourself into now, Beckett?

Chapter 13

BECKETT DIDN'T WANT TO go with Donnie, he wanted to stay with Chloe and her sister, but he didn't have much choice in the matter. Besides, he was curious about what Chloe had said, about the girls below deck.

After fetching another Scotch, Donnie led him downstairs.

Only it wasn't just any 'downstairs,' the dingy undercarriage of a rusted boat. Instead, the luxury that started up above only became more extravagant down here. After entering through a second door, Beckett found himself in an opulent den, complete with leather couches, a glass table in the center of the room, and gilded oil paintings on every wall.

"Take a seat," Donnie instructed. Beckett looked around, annoyed that there were no girls present.

"Where are the ladies?" he asked as he sat on a soft leather couch, sipping on his Scotch.

"That's what I want to talk to you about," Donnie remarked, taking a seat across from Beckett. As he did, Beckett noticed that there was a substantial pile of white powder on the table between them.

Donnie must've noticed his gaze as he quickly added, "Help yourself."

Beckett instinctively reached for the cocaine, but then hesitated. He wasn't an idiot; he knew that Donnie was involved in something greater than stealing a yacht. Donnie was clearly connected, and he'd watched enough mobster movies to know that the last thing you wanted to do was owe someone like Donnie a favor.

In addition to being connected, however, it was clear that Donnie was also very astute.

"No strings attached, Beckett," Donnie said, holding his hands out to his sides. "The only thing I ask is that you sit and hear me out. That's it."

Beckett bit his lip as he contemplated the man's offer. In the end, the temptation was too great and he reached across the table. He used a pink and black business card on the table to make a thin line of coke, then used a rolled-up dollar bill to snort it.

It was good shit, and he felt his pupils dilate immediately as a rush of euphoria flooded his system. It was all he could do not to gasp.

It had been a while since he had done any coke, harkening back to his residency days. It wasn't something that he'd done often, only when he needed a little kick to stay awake, when, he had to pull an all-nighter and Adderall simply wasn't cutting it anymore.

As a physician, he also knew the consequences of what he was doing. But, hell, a bump now and then never hurt anyone, did it?

Beckett leaned back on the couch and took a sip of his Scotch, marveling at how the golden liquid, previously delicious, now tasted like liquid perfection on his tongue.

And this time he did moan, not a long drawn out orgasmic sound, but a quick expression of pleasure.

Donnie's smile grew.

"It is good shit," he said, and Beckett nodded in agreement.

The two of them sat there for a moment without saying a thing, until Beckett started to grow uncomfortable.

"All right," he said. "I agree to hear you out, so shoot."

Donnie leaned forward then, first tucking his satin robe around his waist before interlacing his fingers.

"I've got a bit of a problem, you see."

Beckett raised an eyebrow, and when the man didn't continue, he said, "Hemorrhoids?"

While the smile remained on Donnie's face, something hardened in his eyes.

"I wish it were that simple," Donnie said.

"So what's the problem?" Beckett asked, observing the luxurious interior of what must have been the man's private quarters. Even if the yacht was stolen, as Screech suggested it was, Donnie was doing something right. After all, you didn't have shit this good just laying out on a table and a harem of women to do your bidding if you were a scumbag.

Or maybe these were the very things that made you a scumbag; Beckett couldn't be sure which.

Donnie took a deep breath before answering.

"I've got this problem with my girls dying," he said bluntly.

Chapter 14

SCREECH HEARD VOICES ON the lower level of the yacht but had a hard time making them out. At one point, he thought he heard Donnie DiMarco say something, but this was followed by several giggles that were clearly not of Beckett's making.

Breathing heavily now, Screech moved towards the first door he saw, one that was partway open and poked his head in.

"Beckett?" he whispered.

The only answer was another one of those giggles.

Screech pressed his palm against the door and it swung open several inches. The interior of the room was lit by candlelight, showcasing a large bed covered in red satin sheets. Two completely nude women lay on the bed, their arms beneath one another.

And they were staring at him.

The sight of their breasts, perfectly round and glistening with the faint reflection of sweat by candlelight, made Screech's heart start to race.

"You want to join us?" the woman on the left asked. As she spoke, she uncrossed her legs, giving Screech a clear view of what lay between.

"H-h-have you—have you s-s-seen Beckett?" he stammered. He was aware of the fact that he was sweating now, too, and that the front of his shorts had suddenly become uncomfortably tight.

The girl who had asked him to join them raised an eyebrow.

"I don't know who that is, sweetie, but I'm open to a little role play."

Screech swallowed hard; the lump in his throat had gone from an Adam's apple to an Adam's watermelon in the course of a few seconds.

I have to go… I have to find my friend, he intended to say. But when he opened his mouth, one of the girls rose from the bed and started to walk toward him.

Screech found that he could no longer swallow at all.

"Sure, he does," the woman whispered in his ear. She flicked her tongue against his earlobe and a tremor ran up and down his entire spine.

Before he knew what was happening, Screech was guided to the foot of the bed and the remaining woman on it crawled over to him. A moment later, she started reaching into the front of his shorts.

Screech was lost. He would have spent the night, or two, or forever, with these goddesses if it hadn't been for a voice echoing down the hallway.

It was Beckett, and he seemed angry.

"I—I have to go," Screech mumbled.

The girl on the bed grabbed his shorts and pulled him close.

"You're not going anywhere," she said seductively. As if to reinforce this point, the woman to his left licked his ear again.

Then someone shouted—undeniably Beckett this time— and implementing willpower that he didn't know he possessed, Screech brushed the woman's hand away from his belt.

"I'm sorry, I can't—" the standing woman reached for him again, but Screech spun out of the way and hurried toward the door.

What in god's name am I doing? he wondered absently. *I just turned down two of the most beautiful women I have ever seen... for what? For Beckett?*

An image of Beckett holding the bloody stone flashed in his mind.

The man had already shown that he was more than capable of looking after himself.

But there was a difference between taking care of a confused and exhausted ex-convict like Craig Sloan and dealing with someone like Donnie DiMarco.

Screech muttered a curse under his breath and hurried away from the room before he changed his mind. But with the euphoria, regret, and alcohol coursing through his system, he quickly got lost in the labyrinth that was the yacht's lower level. Instead of finding himself anywhere near Beckett and Donnie DiMarco, Screech found himself standing in front of a thick metal door. Under normal circumstances, Screech would have paid it little heed, but seeing as it was so out of place in this lap of luxury, he was drawn to it. The outer padlock was thick and rugged and very clearly closed. And yet, Screech felt compelled to tug on the lock anyways.

It didn't budge.

Beckett shouted once more, and Screech turned back in the direction of the voice. It sounded like it was coming from nearby. He started to move in that direction but stopped when he heard something from the other side of the door.

Screech hesitated, listening closely for the sound again. When it didn't recur, he started to back away.

That was when he heard it again.

"Help us," a soft whisper reached him from the other side of the thick metal door.

This time, Screech pressed his ear up against the cool metal. The music was still droning on from somewhere above, but while the intervening floors had managed to dampen the sound, it was strong enough to make the metal quiver against the side of his head.

"Help us... please help us."

Screech pulled back.

"Is there... is there someone in there?" he asked stupidly.

The response was as immediate as it was haunting.

"Please, whoever you are, help us."

Chapter 15

BECKETT DID HIS BEST to listen intently, but the cocaine was making it difficult to concentrate and he wasn't sure he was following along.

"I think I'm missing something here, Donnie. Your girls are… dying? Why? Sorry, but, uh, that's all I really got from that five-minute diatribe."

Beckett stared at the man as he spoke, trying to figure him out, trying to figure why the hell a man like this needed *his* help. When Donnie's eyes darted to the considerable pile of cocaine on the table, things began to click into place for Beckett.

But unlike Donnie, he wasn't one for euphemisms, genteelisms, or circumlocution; in his experience, all they led to was confusion and misunderstandings. And he wanted to be very clear about certain things moving forward.

There are girls… trapped below…

"You're talking about your mules, right?" Beckett said, a sour taste in his mouth. "You're using girls to smuggle drugs from wherever you're getting them from and they're dying *en route*? Did I get that right?"

Even though his voice remained calm and even, inside, Beckett's feelings couldn't be more opposite.

Donnie smiled.

"You know, they said you were smart and I knew it from the moment I saw you."

Beckett's eyes narrowed and he took a sip of his Scotch.

They said.

"Who told you about me? How did you know I was a doctor?"

Donnie shrugged and Beckett responded by leaning back on the couch.

Two can play this game, he thought.

"Well, I'm not sure where you got your information from, Donnie, but you've been sadly misinformed. You know, Hippocratic Oath and all that. I'm a doctor—I help people. And whatever you're doing here... I'm not interested. Thanks for the coke and the drinks, but I think I'll be on my way right about now."

Beckett expected Donnie to drop the act and be more direct with what he was proposing, perhaps misinterpreting what Beckett had said as a negotiating tactic, but the man remained silent. He just continued to smile his irritatingly perfect smile with sparkling white teeth peeking out from behind his dark beard.

And this suited Beckett just fine. The last thing he wanted or needed was to get involved in a drug smuggling ring, especially given his recent transgressions.

I found girls below deck...

Beckett clenched his jaw as he started to stand. Could he really walk away from this one, though? After a moment of contemplation, he supposed he could, provided he stayed ignorant to any of the details. After all, it wasn't like he was a caped crusader trying to rid the Virgin Gorda of evildoers.

Craig Sloan had been an anomaly; the man had murdered four people and was about to escape. If he'd gotten away, there was little question in anyone's mind that he would strike again.

Beckett was just doing his due diligence as a contributing member of society by taking out Craig... wasn't he?

With a nod, mostly to himself, Beckett turned his back and started to the door. His steps were surprisingly unsteady, though, and it wasn't from the booze or drugs.

Something inside of him had awoken when he'd bludgeoned Craig Sloan, something that wouldn't easily be put to rest.

"I'm not asking for much, Beckett. You say you want to uphold the Hippocratic Oath? Well here's your chance… some of my girls… well, they get sick and I need a doctor to help me keep them from getting sick if you know what I mean."

Beckett stopped to think this over.

An ounce of prevention is worth a pound of cure. If I take out the source of their sickness, then you won't need my help at all, will you, Donnie.

Beckett looked over his shoulder at the man, who was still smiling.

"Thanks for the offer, Donnie. But I think I'll pass."

And there it was again: the shadow passing over Donnie's face, even though his expression didn't outwardly change.

"But you haven't even heard my terms."

Beckett looked around again, taking in the opulence of the room.

"I may not have a Tony Montana-sized yacht, but I'm doing alright. After all, I'm here in this ultra-exclusive resort, aren't I?"

And with that, Beckett offered his own wry smirk and made his way to the door.

Only to have Donnie's words draw him back again.

"You think—heh—you think that I was offering money in exchange for your services?"

Beckett had already made up his mind not to stop walking no matter what the man said to him, but this comment was so surprising that he faltered midstep.

And when Donnie chuckled, Beckett couldn't help but face the man again.

"No, Beckett, I wasn't going to offer you a single dollar."

The smile slid off Beckett's face.

"What then? A hand job? From one of your girls, I hope, and not your hairy mitts."

Donnie ignored the comment.

"I know what you are, Beckett."

"Yeah, you said that already—you know I'm a doctor, big whoop. You proud of your googling skills, or something? Must be quite the accomplishment with those chubby fingers."

Donnie chuckled.

"No, Beckett. I know what you are, and I know what you *did*."

Chapter 16

SCREECH TRIED THE LOCK again, but despite being old and rusted, it held fast.

There was someone in there—no, there were *people* in there. People locked away in a sweltering room, likely without food or water, running out of air…

Screech's mind continued to race as he looked around frantically for something to break the lock.

I wish Drake was here or even Beckett… they would know what to do.

"Hold on," he said quietly. "Just hold on."

Off to one side sat a large wooden crate, but that too was locked. Beside the crate, he saw what looked like kindling leaning up against the wall. Screech found a piece that was roughly the size of his arm, and maybe a third of its diameter, and hurried back to the door.

"Step back," he said, although he wasn't sure why; he doubted that the kindling would be strong enough to do any damage, let alone blow the whole damn door open.

Screech wedged the piece of wood between the lock shackle and body and started to apply pressure. The shackle seemed to rise a fraction of an inch, encouraging him to pull even harder. There was a loud crack as the wood splintered, sending Screech stumbling into the door.

"Fuck."

The response from inside the room was immediate.

"Help us," several voices replied in unison. "Please, help us. One of the girls… she's sick… please. Help."

Screech shook his head.

I'm trying, he thought. *Goddammit, I'm trying!*

He glanced around again and ground his teeth in frustration when he found nothing that looked strong enough to break the lock.

As much as he disliked the idea of leaving the girls alone, Screech knew that he had no other choice. He just wasn't sure what, exactly, he should do next.

If he could find his way out of the maze that was the lower level of the yacht, he could pretend like nothing happened and seek out the authorities.

But that would mean he would have to get past Donnie DiMarco's goons, and maybe even the man himself while keeping a straight face. He wasn't sure he could do that. Besides, it wasn't even clear that this would be helpful; after all, Donnie had already paid off the cops once. Who's to say he wouldn't just do it again?

The other option was to find Beckett.

Except that was what he'd been in the process of doing before he'd become lost and stumbled across the holding cell or whatever the hell it was.

The third, and least appealing, option was to search the other rooms for something to break the lock. But even if he was successful, then what? It wasn't like he could just tuck the girls, however many there were, under his T-shirt and—*ho-hum*—smuggle them off the boat. What if—

Screech froze. In addition to the sound of the women behind the door, he thought he heard something else: footsteps approaching.

Without thinking, he dove behind the crate and tucked himself into as tight a ball as possible. His heart was racing now, and with every beat, his body seemed to rock back and forth. The sound of blood rushing in his ears was like a tsunami crashing down on his forehead.

Screech squeezed his eyes closed and tried, with limited success, to control his breathing.

"Did the boss tell you how long you are to be in port?" he heard one man ask. "We gotta get the cargo moving — we need to make the exchange soon."

This was followed by the sound of sloshing liquid, like someone pouring water into a bucket.

"No idea. Last time we stopped here, Donnie wanted to stay a week before moving on. All I know is that the shipping crate is waiting and that Mendes is none too happy with Donnie's… uh… *extra-curriculars.*"

"*Ungh*, Mendes. That guy creeps me the fuck out."

"Yeah, no kidding. Just finish mixing the drink and then let's get the hell out of here."

Mendes? Who the hell is Mendes?

This was followed by an inaudible exchange.

"What's with the girls up top, anyway?" the first man asked. "I mean, I ain't complaining or nothing, but are they… you know… part of the, uh, cargo?"

"Better not to ask so many questions. Like I said, rumor has it that Mendes isn't pleased. I think it's best if we just do our job. Speaking of which, is the drink ready?"

"Yeah, ready to go. Just open the — wait. What the fuck's that?"

Oh, shit! The wood!

Screech stopped breathing entirely now. He looked down at his hand and realized that while he still clutched the piece of wood tightly between his fingers, he'd left the broken shards on the ground when he had tried to open the lock.

"There's someone else here," the first man said.

At that very moment, the phone inside Screech's pocket started to buzz.

Chapter 17

BECKETT STUMBLED. HIS FIRST thought was that he'd consumed too much, that the alcohol and coke were messing with his head. After all, there was no way that Donnie knew about... about Craig Sloan. About what he'd done.

Then, as if reading his mind, Donnie's smile widened.

"Oh, don't worry; I hear that the tribunal has cleared you of any wrongdoing. And that's the end of it, right? I mean, it's not as if someone has pictures."

Beckett stared at Donnie in disbelief. When he'd agreed to follow the man below deck, he knew that Donnie was of questionable character. And yet, he'd given the man a pass. It wasn't his job to intervene with a drug smuggler, especially one who was connected. But now, after what Chloe had told him, and what Donnie himself had just said, Beckett was having a hard time finding a reason *not* to kill the man.

He took a deep breath.

Control yourself, Beckett. This is not who you are.

Except that wasn't quite true; a previously self-assured man, all of a sudden, Beckett found himself questioning exactly who he was.

Before Craig Sloan, the most violent thing he'd done was getting into a bar fight when he was still in his teens. And even then, Beckett had just been coming to the defense of one of his friends who had been double-teamed.

Craig Sloan had changed all that.

Beckett felt a familiar tingling in his fingertips and he instinctively balled his fists to force the sensation away.

This was what Donnie wanted; for whatever reason, he was trying to provoke Beckett.

Not yet; a drug smuggler doesn't deserve what happened to Craig Sloan. Only murderers deserved that.

Beckett refused to bite.

"I don't know—"

Once again, Donnie DiMarco dismissed him with a wave of his hand.

"Not to worry, my good doctor. Your secret is safe with me," he gestured to the pile of cocaine on the table. "Enjoy your time off. And feel free to help yourself to more cocaine, drinks, or a lady or two. I'm sure you'll find a way to repay me... *later*."

Beckett squeezed his fists so tightly that his knuckles started to ache. He wanted nothing more at that moment than to pummel Donnie until his smile was rendered a bloody smear.

But he couldn't do that—not yet, anyway. In the back of his mind, however, Beckett had a sneaking suspicion that he *would* repay the man later, only not in the way Donnie thought.

He took another deep breath and relaxed his hands.

"So generous of you," he muttered as he backed out of the room.

So much for an uneventful trip to the Virgin Gorda. So much for staying out of trouble.

Beckett made his way down a narrow hallway and up the stairs in a daze, his mind jumping all over the place as it was apt to do when he was high.

He had barely reached the top landing before he saw Chloe and one of her friends looking over at him. As confused as he was, as buzzed as he was, as *upset* as he was, Beckett was still beholden to his more primal urges. And when Chloe walked over and draped an arm over his shoulder, still clutching one of the coconut drinks, her breath reeking of alcohol and her body swaying to the music, he leaned into her.

"Hey, doctor boy, you want to have a good time?" she asked. Apparently, her concern from an hour ago about finding other girls below deck had diminished to the point of nonexistence. As Chloe hugged him tightly, one of her friends, a woman with long dark hair who was completely topless, approached. She was pretty, not as pretty as Chloe, but gorgeous nevertheless.

"I'm thinking that's a great idea, Chlo," the new girl said.

His mouth suddenly incredibly dry, Beckett leaned over and took a sip from the straw that protruded from Chloe's coconut drink.

His attempt to moisten his mouth and throat failed miserably; the drink was so bitter that it was nearly impossible to swallow. Beckett had had his share of alcohol in his day, including some barely palatable hundred and twenty proof Mexican tequila in his younger years, but this... this was worse. It had the same sting of alcohol but was bitter on the front. Impossibly bitter even.

He shuddered and took the coconut from Chloe despite her protests. Then he turned to face the bartender who was staring at him with his wide eyes. As he did, the topless lady sidled up beside him and rubbed her breasts against his arm.

Beckett freed his arm and tossed the nearly empty coconut at Kevin. It struck the bartender in the chest, and he managed to catch it awkwardly with both hands.

"This is the worst drink I've ever had," Beckett said with a grimace. "So goddamn bitter... the end, it's bitter as all hell."

Chapter 18

FIGHT OR FLIGHT OR freeze are the three instinctive reactions that all mammals share when confronted with a stressful or dangerous situation.

More often than not, Screech enacted one of the latter two. But in this case, whether it was the alcohol, the realization that Donnie was keeping hostages locked in a cell, or just plain exhaustion, he opted for the former.

He burst out of the fetal position and swung the piece of kindling at the closest man's shoulders. When it simply bounced off, Screech realized that he'd made a mistake.

But there was no turning back now. He raised the stick again, but this time the burly man grabbed his wrist before he could swing it. The man squeezed hard and Screech had no choice but to drop the useless piece of wood.

He winced and cried out in pain.

Screech never even saw the man's fist before it connected with his forehead. The blow was so powerful that if it weren't for the fact that his arm was being gripped so tightly, he most definitely would have gone down. Stars peppered his vision and, for several horrifying seconds, Screech thought that he was going to blackout. When it became clear he wasn't going to lose consciousness, part of him wished he had: the man was pulling his fist back again, his knuckles red from the previous impact.

But before he could deliver another blow, a commotion behind them served as a distraction.

Screech's eyes darted in that direction in time to see the metal door swing open violently. From the dark interior, a handful of women burst forth. Unlike those that Screech had seen on the main deck, however, these women weren't wearing string bikinis. On the contrary, they appeared to be wearing filthy rags. Some of them even had what appeared to be blindfolds hanging loosely around their necks.

"Get them!" the man still gripping Screech's arm shouted. "Don't let them get upstairs!"

The other man, the one who had unlocked the door, tried to grab the women, but there were simply too many of them, and they were too desperate for his clumsy hands to find purchase.

The man holding Screech swore and finally released his wrist.

"Get them!" he hollered, his voice rising an octave. "Jesus Christ, *get them!*"

Even though Screech was still reeling from the punch, he had enough wits about him to know that his opportunity for escape was limited. He shoved one of the men out of the way and joined the women's ranks as they bolted down the hallway.

"Get them!"

The bellow was so loud that Screech found himself turning, despite the urgency of the situation. And what he saw made his breath catch in his throat.

Between the shoulders of the goons that were lumbering after them, he saw something that would stay with him forever.

Lying on the floor of the cell, were two women, their eyes open in an empty stare, their mouths and lips covered in a pale white foam.

One of the freed girls bumped his arm and spun Screech around. Horrified by what he'd seen, but knowing that he would soon share their fate if he didn't get moving, he started to pump his legs. His limbs felt like warm Jell-O, but Screech somehow managed to keep up with the malnourished and foul-smelling captives. As he ran, he realized that he'd passed the room with the two women who had tried to seduce him.

I should have just stayed with them, he thought incoherently. *If I'd stayed with them, none of this would have happened.*

But then the girls would still be locked in the dungeon.

Fearful that he would get lost again, Screech stayed close to a woman with long, greasy red hair. Less than a minute later, he found himself at the bottom of a staircase, looking up.

"Hurry, hurry, hurry," Screech cried as he stepped aside, gesturing for the women to climb. The first handful of captives quickly mounted the stairs, and he found himself cringing at the pungent odor of day-old sweat mixed with human feces that they left in their wake.

The next two were slower and the third fell at Screech's feet.

A quick glance behind the fallen woman showed that the two men were nearly upon them. Screech turned his gaze to the stairs and debated just leaving her there and sprinting topside. He hesitated for a full second before making up his mind.

"Get up," he grumbled as he reached down and helped the woman to her feet. She was rail thin beneath her rags, except for her stomach; that was hard and distended. But Screech had no time to think about what this meant. With a gentle shove, he helped her onto the first step.

She regained her strength and did the rest, offering him a quick glance with doughy eyes before ascending out of sight.

"I'm gonna make you—"

Screech didn't even look behind him; his leg simply shot out like a piston. There was a whoosh like a deflating air mattress when his foot connected with something hard.

This time, he didn't look back.

B-yacht'ch's upper deck was sheer chaos. The liberated captives mingled with the drunk, bikini-clad girls, all of whom appeared confused and disoriented. The security guards from the ramp had come onto the boat in response to the commotion, but they didn't appear to know what to do, either.

Screech scanned the crowd for Beckett but couldn't see him anywhere.

"I hope you got out of here, Beckett," he whispered through gritted teeth.

His first instinct was to head toward the ramp that had just been vacated, but when he saw the militia hurrying down the dock, he quickly changed his mind.

Instead, Screech turned in the opposite direction, which almost immediately led him to a dead end.

Coming to an abrupt halt, he placed two hands on the railing and stared at the dark water below. And then, with a deep breath and shouts at his back, Screech hoisted himself overboard.

PART II

Blindfolds and Acid Reflux

PRESENT

Chapter 19

THE LAST THING BECKETT remembered was taking a sip of the bitter coconut drink. He knew that he hadn't been alone, that Chloe and her friend were with him at the time, but that was about it. Only they weren't with him now; the two corpses on the bed were different girls entirely. Who they were, and where they'd come from, was a different story entirely.

A narrative that he wasn't privy to.

He shook his head.

"Look, I have no idea..." Beckett let his sentence trail off. Something wasn't right here.

Aside from the two dead girls, of course.

The militia had stormed into his villa with barely a knock, their weapons drawn. They'd known that the corpses were here before they'd entered.

"Looks like you just couldn't stay out of trouble, could you, my good doctor?" the man with the beard, the only one without a uniform, said with a grin.

And the combination of that smirk and the use of the term 'good doctor' made something inside his head click.

Of course, Beckett thought with a scowl. Bits and pieces of his conversation with this man, whose name slipped his mind, came flooding back.

Enjoy the coke and the girls, I'm sure you'll find a way to repay me later.

It was all a setup; Beckett was supposed to help this man with something that he couldn't recall, and when he'd refused, the man had set him up.

More leverage to get Beckett to do his bidding. Which was...?

"I'm unarmed," Beckett said, raising his hands to underscore his point. It was a redundant statement; after all, he was only wearing a pair of sweaty boxers, but he needed more time to collect his faculties.

"Don't move," the man in front ordered.

Beckett obliged. But while he stood completely still, his eyes drifted about the room, desperately seeking a way out. The door was completely blocked by the armed men, but the window behind him was partly open.

If I can only—

But any hopes of making a mad dash for the window were foiled when one of the men stepped forward and ordered him to put his hands down, a pair of gleaming handcuffs at the ready.

Beckett clucked his tongue and did as he was bid, cringing at the foul, bitter sensation on the back of his tongue.

What the hell was in that drink? He wondered. *Why was it so bitter? Why—*

Beckett groaned as more memories of the night prior started to become clear.

My girls… they keep getting sick, the man with the beard had told him.

You mean the girls that you're using as drug mules keep overdosing?

The bitter drink, the two corpses with the paste in the corners of their lips, the need for Beckett's services… it all made sense now.

But this realization had no bearing on the current situation.

"I can help you. I can help—" *godammit what the hell is his name?*

A pair of hands grabbed his hands and started to push them painfully up the small of his back.

"I can keep your girls from getting sick."

He started to remember his conversation with the bartender, about how this man was no Donnie Brasco, that he was—

Donnie! His name is Donnie!

"Donnie, I can help you," Beckett said as he felt cold metal brush against his wrists.

"Hold on a second," Donnie said.

The man with the cuffs relaxed momentarily, and Beckett didn't hesitate.

He bolted.

Someone shouted something in Spanish, and Beckett somehow made it to the window before the first shot was fired.

The bullet whizzed by his ear, coming within inches of his flesh, just as Beckett propelled his thin body out the window with a dexterity he never knew he possessed. The next two bullets splintered the window frame behind him.

"Don't kill him, you fucking idiots—*don't kill him!*"
Donnie's words followed him into the sun.

Gee, lucky me. I get to live another day. But you, Donnie, I doubt you're going to be so lucky when I'm done with you, Beckett thought as he sprinted as fast as his weary legs could carry him.

Chapter 20

SCREECH HID IN THE water next to the yacht for so long, repeatedly ducking beneath the surface whenever he heard someone above or saw the flicker of flashlights, that he'd become a human prune. Only after the sun started to peek above the horizon and the commotion on the boat above died down did he risk swimming away from the yacht. Several minutes after that, he summoned the courage to make a break toward shore.

Lack of sleep had made his memories untrustworthy, but when he'd poked his head up several times during the night, he'd overheard a conversation between the militia and some of Donnie's men. It sounded as if several of the girls had managed to get away and they were in the process of trying to figure him out what to do with the rest of them.

When Screech eventually made it back to dry land, water-logged and exhausted, he also found himself frozen with indecision. Donnie had the local police on his side, and there was no question that the two goons who he'd gotten in an altercation with would recognize him; after all, he and Beckett had been the only two male guests on the yacht the night prior.

Beckett... I need to find Beckett.

Assuming, of course, that the man had made it off the yacht in the first place. Screech had high hopes; the man had proven himself resourceful many times before.

If his time with ex-NYPD Detective Damien Drake had taught him anything, it was that there were two types of people in this world: victims and survivors. While Beckett most definitely fit into the latter category, Screech was still trying to figure out which group he belonged to.

And, as the old poker saying went, if you're sitting at the poker table for an hour and still don't know who the fish is? Guess what, genius, it's you.

Yeah, well, victim or not, I'm not ready to give up. Not just yet, anyway.

Screech kept his head low as he hurried up the small embankment toward the villas. Sticking to the shade offered by palm trees and rock outcroppings, he somehow managed to keep from being noticed. Being immersed in water for a good portion of the night had brought about a tremendous chill, and he desperately wanted to dry himself off and fetch some new clothes, but he didn't dare head back to the reception area. It was too risky and likely crawling with militia.

He knew that there was a good chance that Beckett's villa would also be overrun by corrupt cops, but he had to make sure that the man was okay before he found a way off the damn island.

But Screech never made it to the villa.

He was partway there when he spotted someone sprinting toward him, a shadow in the sun, the man's legs pinwheeling like a cartoon character's.

The man was running so quickly that Screech had to dive behind an outhouse to avoid being bowled over as much as being seen.

When the man passed by him, Screech realized that he recognized him.

His face was red, bordering on purple, and his hair was slick and flat against his skull, but there was no denying who it was.

His tattooed chest and arms gave him away: it was Beckett.

Screech stepped away from the outhouse and was about to holler after Beckett when he heard a commotion behind the man and slunk back into the shadows.

Two men in uniform were sprinting after Beckett, their own deeply tanned faces red with exertion.

Screech huffed. He wanted to help his friend but just couldn't see how. They were on an island, after all.

An island run by Donnie DiMarco, no less; there was nowhere to run, nowhere to hide.

Screech swallowed hard. He'd seen Beckett backed into a corner before, or, more precisely, sandwiched between two houses.

And that had ended badly for the man who'd confronted Beckett.

Remembering that he had his cell phone on him, he reached into his pocket and pulled it out. But a night underwater had rendered it inoperable.

"Shit," he swore under his breath. He lifted his eyes and watched as Beckett sprinted toward the yacht of all places, the militia hurrying after him. And then, behind all of them was Donnie DiMarco, clad now not in a white, satin robe, but in plaid shorts and a low-cut V-neck T-shirt.

And he was still smirking. The prick was still—

Screech yelped as a hand came down on his shoulder, causing him to drop his cell phone.

Chapter 21

BECKETT WASN'T SURE HOW he managed to get away, let alone where he was headed. He just bowed his head down and kept on running.

His feet glided over a rock pathway, then neatly shorn grass. Gravity propelled him down the gradual slope toward the dock. It made little sense to head back to the yacht, the likely spot where the girls in his bed had met their demise, but his legs just kept on churning.

Beckett couldn't stop, even if he'd wanted to.

Shouts followed him, but they were muted by the blood that rushed in his ears. His first thought was that he could just keep on going until he reached the end of the dock and then dive right in. From there, he would swim until his arms and legs and lungs gave out, hoping by some sheer stroke of luck that someone who wasn't bought and paid by Donnie picked him up.

Beckett shook his head.

That was ridiculous.

His best chance was to hide and hope that Screech came up with something... wherever he was.

The last time he had seen Screech, they'd been busy inspecting the boat, trying to avoid the temptations of a dozen half-naked women. Perhaps he was lying in bed somewhere, covered in a sheen of sweat accompanied by now fully naked women.

Beckett only hoped that in Screech's case, these girls weren't dead.

Thoughts of the dead girls drove Beckett's legs even faster.

He could overlook Donnie's drug-smuggling ways, and maybe even the fact that he had somehow gotten insight into what had really happened with Craig Sloan.

But what Donnie had done to those girls, and the fact that he'd used their bodies to frame him, that was inexcusable.

He had to pay.

Which meant that Beckett wasn't going to leave the island after all. Not until he'd dealt with Donnie, that is.

Instead of continuing toward the dock, Beckett made a sharp left and found himself within range of the bar that he'd frequented the day prior with Screech… before all of the craziness had happened.

Beckett slid around the backside of the bar and then ducked beneath it. Heart still pounding, his lungs struggling to draw a full breath, he relished the bit of shade offered by the chest-high wooden structure. It felt sturdy enough to lean up against but wouldn't stop a bullet.

He heard a shout, followed by his name being yelled on the wind—Donnie DiMarco calling for the good doctor again—but paid it no heed.

He did, however, scold himself for being so stupid. Kevin the bartender had warned him several times to stay away, that Donnie was no good, but he'd ignored the warnings. Beckett was confident in his ability to take care of himself, but never had he thought his meddling would result in the deaths of two drug mules.

How ignorant he was.

Another shout reached him, and Beckett pressed his back even harder up against the bar. In the process, his shoulder knocked a bottle off the shelf. Eyes wide, he juggled it in both hands, knowing that if it smashed to the ground the militia would find him in seconds—if they didn't know where he was already.

With a grunt, he managed to finally grab the bottle. To his surprise, however, it wasn't a bottle of alcohol or even some syrupy mixture; it contained a powder and the label looked pharmaceutical.

Confused, Beckett brought it up to his face and read the label.

Rabeprazole.

Beckett turned around to look at the shelf behind him. There wasn't just one bottle of Rabeprazole within arm's reach, but at least a dozen. This was no over-the-counter treatment for acid reflux; Rabeprazole was a powerful proton-pump inhibitor for the treatment of gastroesophageal reflux disease. In the concentrated, powdered form, it would have to be mixed in a—

An image of a coconut flashed in Beckett's mind, one so vivid that he considered that he might still be high.

Kevin was making the girls on the yacht drink the coconut slurries with Rabeprazole mixed to neutralize their stomach acid.

Which was why he kept saying that the drinks weren't for Beckett or Screech, and why they tasted so goddamn bitter.

Beckett pictured the girls in his bed with foam on their lips and their wide, blank stares.

High doses of Rabeprazole might be able to cause acute liver failure, along with cardiac problems, but Beckett didn't think that overdoses could be fatal, at least not on their own.

But in conjunction with alcohol and cocaine and god knows what else?

It was possible.

More than likely though, it simply didn't work; the shitty baggies that they were using burst inside the mules despite attempts to neutralize their stomach acid. And that explained why Donnie was so intent on getting Beckett involved. A chemist might have been a more appropriate candidate for such a task, but it was hard to find one that you had incriminating photos of.

Beckett slipped the bottle back on the shelf and realized that even though he had spent a good minute or two reading and thinking about the proton-pump inhibitor, he no longer heard either Donnie's voice or the militia's shouts.

His hiding spot wasn't *that* good; there were only so many places on the private island that one could take cover before being found.

With a deep breath, Beckett raised his head just high enough to peek over the bar before ducking back down again.

"What the hell?" he whispered.

Chapter 22

IT WAS ALL SCREECH could do not to scream.

He tried to pull away from the strong grip on his shoulder, but it was next to impossible. He lifted his head and stared up at a bald man with muscles that bulged from beneath a skin-tight T-shirt. His heavily lined face was etched with a frown.

Screech's heart finally decided now was the time to pump, causing his appendages to tingle with the fresh flow of blood. It wasn't Donnie DiMarco or even one of the militia; it was Bob Bumacher, the man who had hired him to find his yacht.

Screech blinked several times to make sure that the hulking man beside him wasn't an exhaustion-fueled mirage.

"What? How did you—so fast—you came..." Screech was having a difficult time putting together a full sentence.

Bob brought a finger to his lips and then leaned out from the shadow of the outhouse. Screech followed his gaze and noted that he was staring at Donnie DiMarco, who was talking to the men in fatigues near the dock that moored the yacht.

At this point, Screech didn't give two shits who actually owned the yacht. All he cared about was getting off the island in one piece. It was time to be a survivor, and maybe save Beckett in the process. No, that wasn't right; *definitely* save Beckett in the process.

"What are you—"

Bob hushed him again and surveyed the scene with more intensity.

Screech felt the need to tell the man that the militia were in Donnie DiMarco's pocket, but something suggested that Bob already knew this.

He'd learned a long time ago that someone who could be influenced by a dollar, could be bought for two.

Considering the gaudy sum that Bob had offered Triple D to find his yacht, finances didn't appear to be an issue for Bob Bumacher... and whoever else was behind him. There was no way that Donnie DiMarco or Bob Bumacher could put together a drug smuggling ring of this magnitude without help. It was logistically impossible.

All I know is that the shipping crate is waiting and that Mendes is none too happy with Donnie's... uh... extra-curriculars.

Screech scratched his chin.

Who in the Sam Hell is Mendes?

It took him a moment to realize that Bob was no longer staring out at the dock and had instead turned his attention to Screech himself.

Screech, fatigued to the point of nearly falling over, lowered his gaze.

Bob put his hand again on Screech's shoulder and gave it a little squeeze.

"You done good, Screech. Now I want you and your friend to stay out of the way for a little while. Keep low and I'll get things sorted."

Finally grateful for someone else to be taking the helm, Screech nodded.

With that, Bob released his grip and stepped out into the light, his massive arms held wide, a smile on his face.

"Gentlemen," he exclaimed. "How nice to see you again. My employer says hello."

Confusion washed over the faces of the men with the machine guns. The only person who didn't look confused, however, was Donnie DiMarco.

That man turned and ran.

Still not sure he fully understood what was going on, Screech turned his eyes away from Bob Bumacher and searched for Beckett.

Bob had instructed him to stay out of the way, but when he caught a glimpse of a frightened-looking Beckett poke out from behind the bar, Screech knew he couldn't do that. Well, he could stay out of the way, but he couldn't stay here. He had to get to Beckett, he had to tell his friend what he'd seen.

About the girls trapped in the cell on the lower level of the yacht.

Beckett would know what to do.

He had to because Screech sure as hell didn't.

Chapter 23

BECKETT CLUTCHED A HALF-EMPTY bottle of bourbon in his hand as he waited for the man to approach. He hadn't seen his face, had only heard his obnoxiously loud breathing, but he wasn't taking any chances.

He had no idea who the white hulk that made his way across the lawn was, but Beckett knew that it would take a lot more than a bottle to bring him down. One of the militia, however, if caught unawares…

On a three count, Beckett leaped to his feet, the bottle held high above his head… only to lower it again.

"Screech? What the fuck?"

But even as he asked the question, Beckett thought he knew the answer. The man looked disheveled, with thick dark circles beneath his eyes. For someone as skinny and young as he was, Screech's skin looked loose and wrinkly. And he was wet; everything about him was wet, from his hair to his soggy runners.

"You sleep with Ariel, or what? What happened to you?" Beckett asked.

Screech's upper lip curled.

"What happened to me?" he exclaimed. "What happened to *you*? One second we're together on the boat, then you're gone, man. I basically slept underwater."

Beckett glanced around nervously and pulled Screech down below the bar.

"Never mind that—we need to get off this island. I don't know how, but we need to get out of here fast. Some shit… *yeesh*, some shit went down last night."

Screech's eyebrows rose up his pasty forehead, but not in a way that suggested concern or more confusion. It was more *knowing...* knowing and scared. Screech was definitely frightened.

"What?" Beckett asked. "What is it?"

Screech shook his head and leaned in close.

"You don't know the half of it, Beckett. I was looking for you on the stupid boat and I made my way downstairs. But I got lost and instead of finding you... I found something even worse."

Interesting choice of words, Beckett thought. When Screech got a far-off look in his eyes, he reached over and shook his arm.

"What, Screech? What did you see?"

Instead of answering, Screech grabbed the bottle of bourbon from Beckett's hand and popped the top. He took a swig, wiped his mouth with the back of his hand, and offered it to Beckett. Beckett sipped and then put the top back on, wincing at the burning sensation in his throat.

At least it's better than coconut, tequila, and Rabeprazole.

Imbued by liquid courage, Screech started to speak again, weaving a tale about finding women trapped in a cell in the bottom of the yacht. When he was done, Screech took the bottle back and had another drink, a triple gulper this time.

Beckett squinted at Screech as he mulled this over.

"Screech... the two girls... the dead ones you saw lying in the yacht. Was one a brunette and the other a blond?"

Screech gave him a queer look.

"I... I think so. It was hard to tell. They were all just so... *dirty.*"

Beckett nodded.

"And their asses? Did they have these asses," he made a circular gesture with his hands, "that you could, like, bounce quarters off of? Big ol' round things?"

Screech recoiled.

"What? What the fuck are you talking about? You think this is a joke, Beckett? *They're dead.* And we will be too if you don't stop messing around."

"I'm not, Screech. Just answer the question: did they have big hard asses?"

Screech looked like he was going to be visibly ill.

"I don't fucking know!" Screech exclaimed. Beckett cringed and ducked even lower.

"Keep your voice down," he hissed.

"I don't know about their asses. They were dressed in rags… filthy things. All I saw was their goddamn dead eyes and the foam around their mouths."

And that sealed it; Beckett had all the evidence he needed.

The girls had died on Donnie's yacht and the man had placed them in Beckett's bed when he'd been passed out.

"Okay, okay," Beckett said, trying to calm his friend who looked on the verge of hyperventilating. He reached out and lifted the bottle of bourbon, encouraging Screech to consume more of the firewater. The man obliged.

"And you? What the hell happened to you? And why was the goddamn army after you?"

Beckett didn't know how to answer; Screech wasn't cut out for this sort of thing and telling him that the girls he'd seen dead in the yacht had ended up in his bed, stripped naked… well, that might just put him over the edge.

Beckett opted for a high-level summary.

"Long story. Basically, Donnie wanted me to help him with his drug smuggling bullshit. I declined, and he set me up."

He could tell by the look on Screech's face that he knew there was more to this story, but thankfully he didn't push it.

"You have your cell phone?" Screech asked, changing the subject.

Beckett looked at himself and held his hands out, showing Screech that he was only sporting his tattooed chest and a pair of boxers.

"Does it look like I have a damn cell phone?"

Screech frowned and pulled his own sopping phone from his pocket.

"I managed to take a picture of the yacht before I spent the night in the water," he began, reaching for the bourbon again. "Managed to get a text off to the guy who hired me to find it."

Beckett waited for the man to finish his drink.

"And?"

Screech lowered his gaze.

"And I don't know how, but he's here."

Beckett raised an eyebrow.

"Here? As in on the island?"

An image of the white hulk flashed in Beckett's mind.

"Yeah, he's here and I don't think he likes Donnie DiMarco very much."

Chapter 24

"**BOB TOLD US TO** lay low," Screech said, peering over the top of the bar. Bob and the militia had since disappeared out of sight, and he hadn't seen Donnie since the man had bolted toward the yacht. "I think... I think that we should listen to him."

Out of the corner of his eye, he saw Beckett frown.

Screech secretly hoped that Bob would just pay off the authorities the way that Donnie had and that everything would be wrapped up with a nice little bow. He and Beckett would then fly back to New York and leave this mess behind them, with only a sunburn and a crazy story that no one would believe for their troubles.

But something told Screech that Beckett wouldn't just let this go—that unlike Screech, he *couldn't* let it go. With a hard swallow, he turned to face his friend.

There was an emptiness to Beckett's pale blue eyes that hadn't been there even yesterday when they had been drinking and joking at the bar.

In fact, Screech had only seen this look once before; when Beckett had been standing over Craig Sloan's fallen body, a bloody stone in his hand.

I should never have told him about the dead girls... I should have just left it at the girls being trapped in a cell.

But Screech couldn't deny the possibility that part of the reason he'd told Beckett was because he had a suspicion of what the man might do. And maybe—just maybe—deep down, he wanted Beckett to take care of Donnie the way he had Craig.

Screech shook his head.

You're just exhausted... what happened with Craig was an accident. Beckett wouldn't... he wouldn't... he's not like that. He's a doctor, for Christ's sake.

"Let's just wait this out," he said. "Wait for things to blow over."

Beckett turned to him then, the same empty look in his eyes.

"Wait for things to blow over?"

Screech waited for Beckett to expand on this, to ask him how he could let the deaths of two girls just 'blow over.' But he didn't. And somehow, this silence was even more powerful than a long, drawn-out discussion of morality and ethics.

Screech cleared his throat and looked away from his friend.

"Donnie would probably just pay them off, anyway," Screech said under his breath, turning his eyes back to the spot where he'd last seen the man with the beard. He knew he was justifying something that hadn't even happened yet, something that most likely would *never* happen, but he couldn't help it.

"How hard do you think it can be?" Beckett said after a long pause.

Screech's brow furrowed as he followed his friend's gaze. Beckett was staring at *B-yacht'ch* moored to the end of the long dock.

"I mean, I stole one in GTA V once. Wasn't difficult."

Screech didn't know much about boats, and less about yachts, but the sheer size of the vessel suggested that it might take at least a half-dozen people to drive the damn thing, let alone park it. But before he could say as much, Beckett was already rising to his feet.

"I have no idea, but I guess we're going to find out," he muttered under his breath.

Chapter 25

YOU'RE GOING TO PAY, Donnie, Beckett thought as he ran. *You're going to pay for what you did to those girls.*

He knew that his plan was risky, suicidal, even, but his fingers had started to tingle and his mind had already been made up.

There was just one thing he had to work out: how to keep Screech out of this. Beckett liked the man well enough, even though he was undeniably annoying, but this was something that he had to do alone.

Unlike the night prior, there were no burly men blocking the private ramp to the yacht, just a simple rope that both Beckett and Screech managed to hop over in a single bound.

In broad daylight, and in the absence of cocaine and alcohol, aside from the small amount of bourbon he'd consumed at the bar, the yacht felt wholly unfamiliar to Beckett.

Not only that, but it appeared as if someone had cleaned up overnight, removing the bar that Kevin had worked at entirely, as well as any evidence of the coconut massacre that had taken place. Beckett still wasn't sure what the bartender's role was in all of this, but he hoped for all of the man's warnings, that he didn't know the details of what Donnie had been up to.

He's here, Beckett thought suddenly. *Donnie's here.*

He didn't know how he knew this, but the closer he got to the staircase leading to the deck below, the surer he became.

"We should find a phone—a phone to call Drake," Screech whispered beside him.

Beckett couldn't tell if Screech was speaking to him or just thinking out loud, but he took the opportunity to put some space between him and his friend.

"There's probably one in the... ugh... cockpit," he offered.

"Then let's go," Screech replied, but Beckett pulled away. He wasn't going to go with Screech; he had something else to take care of. "What's wrong? We should stick together."

Beckett shook his head.

"There's something I have to do," he said.

Screech stared at him for a good ten seconds before finally lowering his gaze.

"Be careful," the man said at last.

Beckett nodded.

"Meet me back here on the deck in ten," he said, moving toward the staircase. "Then we'll figure out a way to get off this damn island."

Chapter 26

SCREECH PUSHED THOUGHTS OF what Beckett was planning to do from his mind as he made his way to the front of the yacht. He was simply too exhausted to wrap his mind around anything.

And thinking about it would do no good at this point.

He passed several empty rooms and, as he did, Screech realized that the vessel was not only squeaky clean but appeared completely deserted. Which was odd, given what had happened on board just last night.

He shook his head and tried to remain focused.

I need to find a phone and call Drake.

There was still the question of *what* he would tell his partner when he finally got a hold of him, but he would deal with that hurdle when he got to it.

The door to the cockpit was ajar and Screech pushed it all the way open, prepared to run should he encounter any of Donnie's men—or were they Bob's now?—inside.

His heart skipped a beat when he realized that there *was* someone inside.

Only Screech didn't run; he froze.

"No, please god, no."

Lying on the floor in front of a panel of knobs and wheels and buttons, was the bartender.

Screech didn't need to check the man's pulse to know that he was dead.

Kevin was on his back, his arms outstretched at his sides. The man's flesh had the pallor of spilled milk, a stark contrast to the deep tan that he had sported when Screech had seen him last. His eyes stared blankly at the ceiling.

Screech swallowed hard, trying to keep the vomit that threatened to rise in his throat at bay.

The only thing that kept him moving, pushing him forward, was a nonsensical mantra that repeated in his mind.

I need to call Drake, I need to call Drake, I need to call Drake...

Screech tilted his head at an odd angle as he entered the cockpit and glanced around, a deliberate attempt not to see Kevin's corpse again.

From just outside the door he'd observed hundreds of tiny switches and dials, but inside... inside, there were *millions* of them.

There's no way I can drive this thing, he thought. But that wasn't his focus anymore.

His focus was calling Drake; it was the only thing that would keep him sane.

Thankfully, a red phone jutted from the side of the desk and Screech went right to it. Without thinking, he picked it up and held it to his ear.

To his surprise, even though he hadn't dialed a number, it was already ringing.

"Coast Guard, what's your emergency?"

Screech blinked once, twice, and then collapsed, his ear still pressed against the phone.

He'd finally lost his battle with exhaustion and sleep deprivation.

"Coast Guard, what's your emergency?" the man on the other end asked again.

Screech's chest started to twitch uncontrollably.

"If you are unable to speak, please send your GPS coordinates."

The phone fell from his hand and dangled from the cord an inch or two above the floor.

And then everything came crashing down.

What started as a thin whine quickly degenerated into body-wracking sobs. Screech buried his face in his hands as the voice on the phone continued to inquire about the nature of the emergency.

What's my *emergency?* What's my emergency? *My whole life... my whole life has become a fucking emergency.*

It was a full minute later that Screech realized that he'd heard another sound in addition to the coast guard's voice: a buzzing from his pocket.

Screech pulled his hands away from his face and reached into his still-damp shorts.

Through tear-streaked vision, he somehow managed to confirm that his phone had come back to life.

And that there was a message waiting.

A message from Drake.

It took him nearly a dozen tries to successfully open the message and when he finally managed, Screech simply stared at it, unable to contemplate a reply, let alone type one.

How did you explain something like this over a text? How did you tell someone that you found yourself on a yacht owned by a drug smuggler, found a dozen girls hidden away in a secret cell, two of whom were dead, and that you'd probably just sent your friend to kill the man responsible?

How in the *fuck* did you explain that?

Screech blinked and read the message a second time.

How's the vacation, Screech? Did you find Bob's yacht?

Chapter 27

BECKETT PASSED THE ROOM that he had done the coke in
with Donnie DiMarco the night prior and glanced inside. Like
the rest of the boat, it too appeared to have been scrubbed
clean of any evidence of last night's debaucheries.

But he had no interest in any of that now. His goal
remained singular.

He looked in several other rooms in the lower level of the
yacht, searching for what Screech had described as a door that
belonged in a back alley in New York and not on a luxury
yacht. But all he saw were neatly made beds and polished
dressers.

Just when Beckett was considering going back topside, he
turned a corner and nearly tripped over an empty pallet.
Made of worn wood, he'd seen dozens of them stacked behind
grocery stores back in New York.

Needless to say, it didn't fit *B-yacht'ch*'s general decor.

There was also the smell: the faint lavender scent that
seemed to permeate all of the empty rooms was gone. In its
place was a hint of vinegar.

Heroin, Beckett thought. During his tenure as the Senior
Medical Examiner for the NYPD, he'd come across many an
overdose victim. And the times when the drug of choice had
been heroin, the cadavers had always had a unique vinegar
smell to them, as if their last meal had been a bag of salt and
vinegar chips.

Raising his eyes, Beckett saw the door next, nearly exactly
the way Screech had described it: made of thick metal, it was
worn and tarnished, but still looked sturdy. The padlock was
tightly fastened, but Beckett could see splinters of wood on

the ground, evidence that Screech had tried, and failed, to pry it open.

His heart racing now, Beckett looked around for something more useful than a piece of timber to break the lock. It appeared that whoever was in charge of cleaning up the yacht must have taken a break just outside the door, or maybe they'd gone to fetch more supplies. Either way, Beckett found a crowbar leaning up against the wall and beside that, a yellow X-Acto knife. He slipped the knife into the waistband of his boxers, then picked up the crowbar, taking a moment to get used to the weight, its heft. Clutching it in both hands, he moved to the door next.

Beckett tapped the metal door twice with the curled end and waited.

After the metallic echo subsided, he heard a voice.

"Hello?"

Beckett didn't answer. If there had been any part of him that had doubted Screech's story, any part that believed the girls in his bed had died by accident, that Donnie himself was just a victim, the strangled reply vanquished his final doubts.

Donnie had to pay. Of that, Beckett had no doubt.

Without hesitation, he took the crowbar and wedged it in between the lock and then leaned on it. At first, nothing happened—the lock was old, but the clasp was thick. But he didn't give up. With a grunt, Beckett pressed all his weight down on the crowbar.

There was a metallic grinding sound, followed by a snap. Although the clasp hadn't come completely free, all it took was a few twists with his hand and Beckett managed to slip it off.

No sooner had he pulled the lock free, was the door pushed open from the inside.

Beckett jumped out of the way, holding the crowbar in one hand while moving the other to the X-Acto knife in his waistband.

A woman clad only in a string bikini bolted out of the room. Her eyes were streaked with black makeup and her hair was a mess, but for an instant, Beckett thought that it was actually Chloe.

But when she didn't stop and he got a really good look at her, Beckett realized that it wasn't Chloe, but one of the many women from last night who looked just like her.

He was about to step inside the cell when three other women pushed by him. He stepped aside and allowed them to pass.

His heart had been racing before, but now it felt as if his blood had started to boil. He couldn't wrap his mind around what these women had felt, locked in a dark room, not knowing when, if ever, they'd be let free again.

Beckett watched as the women made their way down the hall and out of sight. When they were finally gone, and he was convinced that no other women were inside the makeshift cell, he stepped inside.

The interior was the complete opposite of the rest of the yacht: the floor appeared to be made of concrete, as did the walls. There were stains on both, dark stains that looked like oil or some other equally viscous substance. Near the back was a bucket that, even from his distance, Beckett knew what it was used for.

The smell gave it away.

Off to one side was another wooden pallet, just like the one outside the room, only this one wasn't empty; it was stacked waist high with bricks of yellow powder.

And then there were the dozen or so loops of black fabric, gags or maybe blindfolds, several of which had splotches of rust-colored stains on them like those on the wall.

His blood still boiling, Beckett pulled the X-Acto knife from his waist and clutched it tightly, his thumb on the slide.

Yeah, Donnie DiMarco was going to pay alright.

Just as he started to back out of the room, someone spoke from behind him and, for the second time in as many minutes, Beckett froze.

"I told you that I needed your help, Beckett, but you just wouldn't listen."

Chapter 28

SCREECH STARED AT HIS cell phone for a long time before replying. He'd managed to remain relatively calm and sane up to this point by convincing himself that Drake could solve all his problems, but now he realized how foolish that idea was.

After all, Drake had his own problems to deal with, ones that rivaled, or even exceeded, his own. It wasn't fair to bring him on board with this.

Screech swallowed hard and wiped the tears from his eyes.

You're a fucking adult, Screech. Why don't you start acting like one?

He read the message one final time before typing a perfunctory text.

Found the yacht and let Bob know.

He quickly followed this with a second.

Everything's all good.

It hurt him to lie to his friend, but it wasn't the first time, and most definitely wouldn't be the last.

He wondered briefly how many times you had to do things that were against your character, contrary to what you believed in before you were just kidding yourself; before *that* was who you actually were.

Screech was about to slip the phone back into his pocket when it buzzed with Drake's reply.

Remember what Bob said; discretion. I'll see you when you get back.

With a sigh, Screech rose to his feet.

Discretion… something tells me that this is going to stick with me for a long, long time.

He swore then looked out the cockpit windshield.

At first, he simply stared out at sea, watching as the waves broke fifty feet from shore. He almost got lost in this hypnotic scene and might have even fallen asleep for a few seconds, before he heard something.

The sound of people making their way down the dock.

Bob Bumacher was striding forward, a stern look on his pink face, two militia walking briskly behind him.

Screech glanced down at the dials all around him and shook his head.

Steal this thing? Really? I'd have better luck operating a plasma torch without getting burnt.

It occurred to him then that stealing the yacht was probably never the actual plan, but rather just a way for Beckett to get rid of him.

And Screech knew exactly why the man wanted to be alone.

"Fuck," he said, rubbing his eyes.

He had to do something.

As much as he despised Donnie DiMarco and what he'd done, he couldn't let Beckett go through with it.

He couldn't allow a repeat of Craig Sloan.

Once you went there… you could never come back. And Screech thought he might still be able to save his friend.

I've got to stop him, he thought as he forced his tired legs to make him move again.

Chapter 29

"FANCY MEETING YOU HERE," Beckett said with a sneer.

Donnie smirked and waved the gun in his hand back and forth.

"You did this... you brought that man—Bob Bumacher— here, didn't you?" Donnie said, still smiling.

Beckett said nothing, but he slipped the X-Acto blade back into the waistband of his boxers as he raised the crowbar in his other hand as a distraction.

Donnie's eyes followed the crowbar.

"Yeah, you did. I don't know why I thought we could work together, that you could help me—that we could help each other. I should have known that Ken Smith would get involved."

Beckett tried to keep his composure, but the mention of New York City's Mayor threw him for a loop.

Ken Smith? Is he involved in this, somehow? More importantly, what does this have to do with me?

"See, the thing is... I think we were *both* set up. I can see it in your face, good doctor: you didn't even know that he was behind you coming here. What, you think it's a coincidence that the moment you arrive, Bob shows up as well?"

Beckett's brow furrowed.

He thought back to his meeting with Internal Affairs after what had happened with Craig Sloan. Not only had they decided not to press charges against Beckett, but they'd also refrained from reporting the incident to the College of American Pathologists. Instead, they'd suggested that he take a vacation.

And, lo and behold, Beckett's friend had called not twenty-four hours later, letting him know that if he ever wanted to get away from the city, that he could stay at the very exclusive resort on the Virgin Gorda...

Beckett shook his head, wondering why he hadn't seen the connection earlier.

He wasn't sure if Ken Smith was behind this, but the fact remained that *someone* wanted him here, someone who wanted him to meet up with Donnie DiMarco.

Whether their intention was for Beckett to help Donnie with his particular problem, or to do what he'd done to Craig Sloan, was unknown.

Either way, Beckett had already made up his mind.

"It doesn't matter why you and I are here, only that we are," he said at last.

The smile slid off Donnie's face.

"Oh, it matters alright, it matters a great deal. I, for one, am nobody's puppet. I'm Donnie DiMarco, for Christ's sake. Now, why don't you drop that crowbar and step forward?"

Beckett let go of the crowbar and it clanged loudly on the concrete floor.

"You're going to pay for what you did," Beckett said through clenched teeth. His fingers were tingling again and his heart had started to race, not with fear, however, but with something else.

Excitement.

Donnie gave him a funny look.

"Oh, it's like that, is it? You're some sort of caped crusader, now? Don't forget that I know what *you* did—I know that you killed Craig Sloan. I know that you bashed his skull in with a rock. I know this because the same people that made sure you came to this island told me about you. And you wanna know what the funny thing is? I came to you for help, to help my girls so that they *stopped* dying. But that asshole Ken and his men? They're the real bad guys, the worst of the—"

A spindly figure suddenly appeared behind Donnie, something round and cylindrical clutched in two hands.

Donnie never saw the blow coming.

Screech drove the butt end of the fire extinguisher into the side of the man's head. His eyes rolled back and he staggered for a moment before collapsing to the ground in a heap. The gun skittered across the floor and when it bumped against the wall, Beckett came to his senses. He dashed over to Donnie, slipping the X-Acto knife from his boxers as he did.

"W-we have to get out of h-h-here," Screech stuttered. "B-b-bob's coming."

Beckett ignored his friend as he hovered over Donnie's fallen body. The man's eyes were fluttering and he was moaning between labored breaths. There was a trickle of blood coming from his temple, which made his hair look even darker.

Beckett leaned in close.

"I told you I'd make you pay," he whispered in the man's ear.

The thing about being a doctor, especially a pathologist, is that you implicitly knew the most efficient methods to kill someone; all you needed to do was reverse engineer what they taught you in med school, mainly how to save someone's life.

When a patient breaks their femur, the first thing you do is make sure that their femoral artery is intact. If it's ruptured or damaged in any way, you need to stem the bleeding quickly, else the patient will bleed out in about five minutes.

The sound of footsteps above provided the perfect distraction. After confirming that Screech's eyes had drifted upward, Beckett slipped the knife into his hand and extended the blade a quarter inch. Then, with his free hand, he hiked up the right leg of Donnie's shorts.

All it took was one small, deep incision, and Donnie's pale inner thigh started to turn red.

Beckett lowered the man's shorts again and they immediately started to darken as they sopped up his blood.

"Screech? Help me get Donnie upstairs," he said quickly. "We need to get him upstairs before anyone finds him."

Chapter 30

SCREECH PASSED A FIRE extinguisher on the way to the lower deck and, for some reason, he picked it up. And then, when he eventually found Donnie holding Beckett at gunpoint, he was glad he had: without thinking, he drove the bottom of the tank against the side of the man's head. Screech had never hit someone in the head with anything, let alone a metal fire extinguisher, and wasn't sure how much strength to put behind it. But Donnie had a gun, which meant that not enough power would likely mean getting shot and maybe even killed.

He gave it his all, and Donnie dropped like a stone.

As Screech struggled to catch his breath, he heard footsteps upstairs. Despite only being distracted for thirty-seconds, maybe even less, Beckett had done... *something*... during that time. In his periphery, Screech caught a flurry of movement, but when he looked back his friend appeared the same as before: hovering over Donnie, staring down at the man with a loathsome expression on his face.

But while Beckett appeared the same, Donnie had changed: for one, the man's bladder appeared to have let go and his shorts had started to turn dark.

His eyes were also different; the alpha look, the steely gaze, that Screech recalled from yesterday in the lobby when Donnie was ordering the receptionist around, was gone.

Beckett was the alpha now, of this, Screech had no doubt.

But there was no time to think about what any of this meant, or literally anything at all that had happened over the past twenty-four hours. It wouldn't do either him or Beckett any good if they were found with the unconscious man only a few feet from the makeshift cell.

Screech wrapped one arm around Donnie's waist, while Beckett did the same on the other side. Together, they hoisted him to his feet, and then they dragged Donnie to the stairs. It took some effort—Donnie was no small man—but they eventually managed to haul him up to the upper deck.

It was only when they made their way around the staircase that Screech noticed his hands were stained with blood.

Beckett did do something... he... what? Cut him? Stabbed him?

The strange thing was that the only injury Screech could see was the trickle of blood from where Donnie had been struck with the fire extinguisher.

"Go get Bob," Beckett ordered in a calm voice. "Intercept him."

Screech blinked.

"What are you... what are you gonna do?" he whispered.

Beckett looked to the water over the side of the railing before answering.

"Donnie is going to have an accident," he said simply. Then he turned back to Screech and unexpectedly shouted. "Go, Screech! Go! Don't let Bob come over here."

Screech blinked again and then took to action, sprinting toward the other side of the yacht. Only before he turned the corner, he chanced a look back over his shoulder.

Beckett was hovering over Donnie's body again and he was saying something. Donnie only moaned in reply and Screech realized that the blood on his hands had come from the man's right leg. He also noticed a red smear leading from the staircase to where Donnie now lay.

Yeah, Screech thought, his stomach suddenly tight. *Beckett did that. I don't know how, or where, exactly, but he cut him.*

And then, as Screech watched in sheer horror, Beckett reached down and wrapped his arms around Donnie's waist.

His friend's lips moved as they pressed against Donnie's ear, but from his distance, Screech couldn't make out any words.

And then, without ceremony, Beckett hoisted the man to his feet and tossed him over the side.

Screech wasn't sure why, but he reached into his pocket then and pulled out his cell phone.

Maybe it was instinct, or maybe he was just continuing with orders from Ken Smith, but either way, Screech snapped several photographs, first of Beckett, then of the bloody deck, and finally of Donnie DiMarco in the water.

The shock of being submerged must've caused the bearded man to come to, because in the photograph that Screech captured, Donnie's arms were outstretched, reaching toward the surface, his eyes wide.

Only he was too weak to swim.

The sound of someone approaching caused Beckett to turn, and Screech quickly ducked behind a pillar. Only he wasn't quite fast enough.

Beckett had seen him, Screech was sure of it. And this realization sent a shiver of fear up and down his spine.

Chapter 31

"DONNIE HAD AN ACCIDENT," Beckett said with a straight face.

Bob Bumacher's eyes drifted to the blood-streaked deck boards, then to the red smears on Beckett's bare chest.

Beckett didn't falter: he locked eyes with the muscular man across from him, wondering what he was going to say.

But instead of asking for details, an explanation, Bob simply nodded.

"The world is better off without him."

The choice of words struck a chord with Beckett and reminded him of one of the last things that Donnie had said.

About how Bob Bumacher was worse than him.

But that asshole Ken and his men? They're the real bad guys...

Bob turned to Screech next.

"Well, we better get this place cleaned up. Then do you guys want a lift back to the mainland? You can hop on a flight to New York from there."

Screech, who somehow looked paler than he had even after spending a night in the water, nodded.

"What about the bodies? The ones Donnie planted in my bed?" Beckett asked.

Bob glanced over his shoulder at the militia that were standing on the ramp leading up to the yacht.

One bad dude is put out of business, but business stays the same, Beckett thought unexpectedly.

"The girls that Donnie killed? It looks like he paid for that. I wouldn't worry about the rest."

Beckett nodded again.

There was a coldness to Bob Bumacher, one that put him on edge. Again, he was reminded of Donnie's final words.

Beckett turned his eyes to the water and stared at the bubbles that rose to the surface, the last vestiges of Donnie's existence.

If Bob truly was a bad man, then his day would come.

His day would come just like it had for Craig Sloan and Donnie DiMarco.

Epilogue

BECKETT CLOSED HIS EYES and took a deep breath. In his mind, he saw Donnie's face several inches below the surface of the water.

He deserved to die, Beckett told himself with a nod. *Donnie might have come to me for help, but the fact remains that he was responsible for the deaths of those two girls and countless others.*

With a sigh, he took a seat on the edge of his bed and removed a leather case from the bedside table.

Inside, Beckett found a pencil with a sewing needle embedded on the end. With the precision of a surgeon, he wrapped a length of thread around the end of the needle, then dipped both into a small container of ink.

Using a small vanity mirror, he observed the tattoo that ran horizontally across his ribs beneath his right arm.

Inhaling sharply, he brought the stick and poke contraption to his skin.

As Beckett tattooed a second line beneath the first, he repeated the name of his most recent victim under his breath.

"Donnie DiMarco… Donnie DiMarco…"

When he was done, he ran a finger over the first line.

"Craig Sloan," he whispered. Then he traced the new, red and raw tattoo. "Donnie DiMarco."

It wasn't remorse that Beckett felt in that moment, but something else entirely: *Relief.*

Both men had deserved to die and, without them, the world was a better place.

But the world still wasn't perfect; there would always be room for improvement.

And with this realization, Beckett felt a new emotion wash over him: *excitement.*

END

Author's Note

I WROTE BITTER END as a stand-alone prequel to the Dr. Beckett Campbell Medical Examiner series because he flat-out deserved it. The truth is, Beckett isn't new; he's been pulling heavy weight in the first five books of the Detective Damien Drake Series. And, *technically*, BITTER END slides in nicely between Books 3 and 4 in that series (Download Murder and Skeleton King, respectively). In fact, I had initially conceptualized this book as a companion to the Drake Series and had considered giving it an obnoxious .5 number (Drake 3.5), even though Amazon doesn't technically let you do that. But, in the *bitter* end, I felt like I was shortchanging Beckett. After all, this isn't a Drake book; it's a Beckett book, one that you can enjoy even if you're completely new to my thriller books.

One thing I particularly love about being an indie author is the ability to write stories that weave characters from my multiple series' together. I've done this with my horror books (The Haunted, Insatiable, and Family Values Series') and I often get emails from you guys telling me how much you enjoy when I do this. I plan on continuing this trend with my thriller series', as well (Drake, Adams, and Campbell). Another great aspect of being an indie is that if one of my characters really gets stuck in my head, I have the freedom to give them the attention they deserve. This is exactly what happened with Dr. Beckett Campbell. I *thought* that he was just going to pop in and out of the first few Drake books and be gone, but like that fungus you got back in High School, goddammit, he just won't go away.

Instead of fighting him, I made him my friend. A friend who has his own series—one that's just getting started.

Speaking of which, ORGAN DONOR, the first official book in the series, is up right now!

As always, if you've enjoyed the BITTER END, please leave a review on Amazon. And if you want to read up on Beckett's origins, head on over to my author page and dive into the Detective Damien Drake series.

You keep reading and I'll keep writing.

Best,
Pat
Montreal, 2018

CPSIA information can be obtained
at www.ICGtesting.com
Printed in the USA
LVHW111528020422
715143LV00019B/177